MW00895651

Better in Time

Mel Henry

Karen —
Happy reading!
— ♡,
Mel

Better in Time

Time After Time series, volume 2

a follow-up novella to *Distance and Time*

by

Mel Henry

Copyright © 2015 by Mel Henry.

All rights reserved. By purchase, you have been granted the non-exclusive, non-transferable, right to access and read the text of this book. No part of this book may be reproduced, transmitted, downloaded, decompiled, re-engineered, scanned, or distributed in any printed or electronic form without permission. Please do not participate in or encourage piracy of copyrighted materials in violation of the author's rights. Purchase only authorized editions.

This book is a work of fiction. Names, characters, places and incidents are either products of the author's creation or are used fictitiously. Any resemblance to actual events, locales or persons, living or dead, is entirely coincidental.

Cover design by Kim Crecelius

Formatting by Graphic Expressions

ISBN 10: 1508993556

ISBN 13: 978-1508993551

Dedication

This book is dedicated to my boyband sisters

For the loyalty you show to the guys who brought us together, and the mutual respect that has cemented our sisterhood over the last thirty years, I thank you. It's only through knowing you that I'm able to create the characters I do and make them realistic and loveable. I hope that you're able to see a small part of yourselves in each of my stories, and that because of that, you let your inner teenager dream a little bit about what might have been.

Foreword

by Jeff Timmons, founding member of 98°

It is an honor for me to write the foreword to Melanie's book. I've known Mel as a loyal fan, and now friend, for the past few years. She's been a support system for my music and other projects, and I've been blessed to have her in my life.

I was surprised to have learned that she is an author. I was blown away by her first work, *Distance in Time*, and am even more impressed with *Better in Time*.

Better In Time is centered around Josh, a former pop star turned actor who is searching for that elusive "true love". *Better in Time* peels back the superficial layers that surround and encompass celebrities, and delves into Josh's struggle between his relationship with whom he feels is his soulmate—Carly—and the woman who has truly given Josh her heart—Abby.

Having an understanding of weeding through façades to get to the truth in a world of fame, Mel does a tremendous job of describing the tensions, emotions, and fears that Josh cycles through.

Better in Time is all about heart, which doesn't surprise me when you get to know the source of the work—my friend, Melanie.

Prologue

December 1993

"I can't believe you're strong-arming me into this, Greg," I grumbled. "Carly's never going to go for this."

"Quite frankly, I don't care what Carly's going to go for, Josh. This has absolutely nothing to do with your little girlfriend." Greg Matheson stood at the end of the board room table with his arms crossed, sporting a smug look on his face. His expensive suit and veneered smile didn't intimidate me much but I knew to pick my battles. Years of experience in the music business had taught me that much.

Our manager, Pete Shepherd, had hired Greg as our new public relations guy a few months ago. None of us were all that fond of him, but to his credit, he had a proven track record for success. According to Pete—that's what mattered. I hoped so because his cocky attitude made every suggestion feel more like a pissing match than a business decision.

"Josh," Pete said in his usual fatherly tone. "I think it's a good idea for many reasons. With Jenna opening for you guys next month, it will help boost her career and honestly..."

"It'll save ours," Bobby grumbled as he flopped back into the chair, flinging his arm over the back of it.

He was right; we all knew it. Ever since Seattle's grunge music hit the scene, our album and ticket sales had taken a blow. We tried changing our sound a little to make it sound less pop and more rock, had a stylist come in to revamp our wardrobes and haircuts, but it wasn't enough: we needed something bigger. Greg, apparently, thought this was it.

I was the lead singer for a group called South Station Boyz. I along with my bandmates: Marc Reyes, Dave Butler, and Bobby Callahan, had built our group from the ground up. And now we were sitting by, helplessly watching it crumble. Linking me romantically to this one-named, teen, pop star was a last-ditch effort to keep us in the press. I knew why Greg and Pete wanted to do this; it made sense. I just didn't want to lose Carly because of it.

"So why can't Dave do it?"

"Dude, don't drag me into this shit. I got a baby on the way," Dave argued. "You want Lynda to cut my nuts off?"

"Bobby?" My voice teetered on the edge of desperation.

"No way, man," he answered, shaking his head. "I'm dippin' into enough honey, already."

"Josh, you're the only one," Pete said. "Dave can't desert a pregnant woman, Bobby's too old—sorry, Bobby—and Marc's . . . well, that's not an option."

I glanced over at Marc who clenched his jaw, staring at the table intently, ignoring eye contact with all of us. For someone who worried about the public finding out his sexual orientation, he couldn't have worked harder at fueling rumors if he tried.

"Why not?" I countered, having decided to stir the pot. If I couldn't win the war, I could take a couple of casualties with me, at least. "Why can't Marc take one for the team? He's the only one who's unattached right now. This is bullshit."

"I'm not doing it, Josh," Marc snapped.

"What's the matter, Marc?" I barked in return. "God forbid the whole world finds out that you're gay."

"Go fuck yourself, McCarthy!" Marc stood up so fast, his chair fell backward, as he practically lunged across the table at me.

"Whoa man!" Bobby jumped up and put a hand on Marc's chest. "It ain't worth it. Just stop—*both* of you." He turned his head and looked at me. "C'mon, cut him some slack. You know this ain't easy for him."

"Yeah, well he does this Jenna thing or I'm gone." My words fell out of my mouth before I could catch them. Surprisingly, in the split-second moment after I said it, I realized I meant it. I'd had it. I was done fighting for air time on the radios. I was done fighting the bad press. I was done fighting with my bandmates. I was just *done*.

"What?" Pete's voice tinged on the edge of panic.

Greg butted in, "Don't be a dick, Josh. We're sticking to the plan. You're not walking. You're going to do what you're told. You're going to stop being a pain in the ass."

He was right. It went down exactly the way he said it would. I was romantically linked to Jenna and it still didn't save our careers.

And I still lost Carly.

She believed me when I told her it was a publicity thing. And to her credit, she stuck with me despite the press declaring my connection with Jenna and numerous pictures to back it up. But with all the touring, Carly's school schedule, and my inability to focus on our relationship, we just couldn't make it work.

It was the one thing in life I truly regretted.

Chapter 1

May 2003

I stood amidst the crowd of travelers, watching Carly until her tearful face finally turned away from me as she retreated toward the doors. I was oblivious to the people around me, only thinking about running after her to tell her we were making a mistake—that this decision wasn't worth it. But I'd already signed the contracts with the network for *Flatline,* a new primetime medical drama, whose cast I would be joining for the fall season. Backing out then would've cost me millions, as well as killed my acting career altogether. Besides, Carly and I had already canceled all the wedding arrangements: the church, the DJ, the caterer, the bakery. I suspected that Carly would burn her dress in effigy. I was also fairly certain that my mother would never forgive me: but what was done was done. I sighed, looking down at my watch then back up at the doors as Carly's head bobbed out of sight. It was too late to change anything.

I checked two bags and threw my backpack over my shoulder, making my way through security. I immediately hit the airport bar and ordered a double. By the time I boarded the plane an hour later, I had a decent buzz. Halfway through my flight, I was nearing full-on drunk.

I hadn't gotten totally shitfaced since South Station Boyz broke up in the mid-nineties. I spent a good portion of that year trashed, bedding as many women as I could and doing enough blow to make Kurt Cobain look like a fucking Boy Scout. To be honest, most of it is a blur and thankfully, since we were "nobodies" at that point, the tabloids never caught wind of all the shit I was doing to my body.

I took the last swig of my drink and swirled the ice around in my glass. I didn't need another refill, but I didn't want to think about Carly either. The scotch numbed my pain and I liked it. I raised my glass at the flight attendant when she made eye contact and she came over quickly.

"I'm sorry, sir," she whispered politely. "I can't serve you any more alcohol on this flight. The airline has a limit. May I get you something else? Coffee or soda, perhaps?"

Her blonde hair was pulled back in a tight knot at the back of her head and it exposed her long, thin neck, which was more like an arrow to the cleavage that peeked out of her uniform. She was tall and had long legs, too. Back in the dark days, I'd have had her pushed against the lavatory wall in minutes, pounding away. But now, all I could see was Carly's face. I snapped out of my daze and shook my head.

"No, thanks."

"All right. If you change your mind, just push that button," she said, her red lips parting slightly and framing her bright white smile.

Carly had a bright white smile. And red lips too—at least after we'd been kissing for a while. I missed her. Fuck, what kind of idiot was I?

I looked up but Blondie was already turned around and making her way back toward the front of the plane. I jammed the button to call her back and fidgeted in my seat until she returned.

"I need to get off the plane," I said when she came back.

"I'm sorry, sir?"

"I need to get off this plane," I repeated a little more loudly, tugging at the seat belt and not succeeding at unfastening it. "I made a huge mistake and I've got to get back to New York."

"Sir," she said. "I'm sorry. You're going to need to keep your belt fastened. We're experiencing some turbulence and the pilot has turned on the 'Fasten Seatbelt' sign. You can't get up."

"Uggh . . . fine," I reluctantly agreed. "But, the pilot has to turn around. I *have* to get back to New York."

"I understand. Perhaps when we land in Los Angeles, we can find you a return flight." She flashed that smile again. Her demeanor was unnervingly calm. I wanted her to be as upset as I was. I wanted her to storm the cockpit and demand they turn the plane around.

The man sitting beside me gave a snort and shook his head before he turned toward the window, dismissing me and my problem. *Asshole.*

Blondie patted my shoulder and I slumped back in my seat. I was stuck.

At some point over the Rockies, I must've either fallen asleep or passed out because I opened my eyes when I heard the pilot come over the loud speaker announcing our descent into LAX. He rattled off time and temperature, but I paid him no mind. I was still a little dizzy and my neck throbbed in pain from the awkward angle at which my head had rested the last hour or so.

I massaged the knot at the base of my skull. The scotch had been a bad idea. Unfortunately, it seemed like bad ideas were all I could come up with anymore. Leaving New York, calling off the wedding, and drinking myself stupid were all bad ideas. Maybe I'd get lucky and they'd kill my character off in the first couple episodes of the show. Then I could move back and tell Carly I was a fucking idiot. She'd forgive me, we'd get married and by this time next year, we'd be on our way to giving my mother more grandchildren.

There was only one problem with that.

I'd read my contracts. I was there for at least sixteen episodes. That meant months in California. I wouldn't resurface until Christmas, if I was lucky. Carly wouldn't be so forgiving by then. And we sure as hell wouldn't be married and making babies. The realization was enough to make me want another drink.

"Hi, this is Carly. I can't get to my phone right now, but if you'll leave a message, I'll get back to you as soon as I can. Thanks!"

I hung up the phone and threw it against the couch. Growling out loud, I folded my fingers and braced my hands on the top of my head as I paced the living room trying to calm down.

I'd been in Los Angeles for a month and other than a couple of brief conversations the week I arrived, I hadn't talked to Carly at all. I called her at home, at work and on her cell. Dozens of messages were left, but she wasn't returning my calls. This was killing me. I had to know what was going on—what she was thinking—if she was okay. Only one person would have the answers: Alejandro.

Alejandro Cruz was Carly's best friend and had been since they were kids. My friendship with him developed when he helped me surprise her for their senior prom. We kept in touch over the years, and Alex had actually been the one to help me get off the booze and drugs. He drove me to rehab and stayed with me for a couple weeks after I got out. To my knowledge, he had never told a soul—including Carly. He was one hell of a guy to have in my corner. I knew he'd be able to find out how she was even if she wasn't returning my calls.

I ran over to the couch and rooted through the pillows until I found my phone. Pushing Alex's number on speed dial, I turned down the television and waited.

"Well hello, Joshua," he answered on the second ring. "To what do I owe the honor of this phone call? Is it Christmas already?"

Sarcasm was the only language Alex spoke most of the time and I knew this was his way of punishing me for being so out of touch lately.

"Hey, Alex."

"You don't call me for a month and all you can give me is a 'Hey Alex'?"

I groaned. He wasn't going to make this easy.

"I'm sorry, man," I said. "You're right. I should've called sooner. I'm a schmuck, and I apologize."

After a long pause, Alex gave a slight chuckle.

"All right, I forgive you. How are you?"

"Miserable," I admitted. "Have you talked to her?"

"Seriously, Josh?" I heard him blow out a long breath and the background noise on his end went silent. "You're interrupting me during *Queer as Folk* to talk about Carly?"

I didn't know what the hell "queer-ass folk" was, but having heard far too many stories about what Alex and his boyfriend did behind closed doors, I was sure I didn't want to know.

"I'm sorry, but I'm freaking out, man," I explained, ignoring his question. "She's not answering her phone, she won't return my messages and her office just says she's out. I have to know what's going on!"

"You're a mess," Alex replied. "She's fine. She's depressed as hell, working a thousand hours a week to take her mind off of you and most likely finding solace in the bottle, but she's fine."

I let out a small breath of relief.

"If she's so fucking unhappy without me, why won't she call me?" I was ashamed at how desperate I sounded.

"Do you really want to know the answer to that?"

Did I?

"Yes?" I replied, still not sure I wanted to know.

"She wants to get over you, Josh." Alex's tone had gone from terse to kind, almost apologetic. "Not to bring up bad juju, but you broke her heart once before. Remember? It took her over a year to get back to being herself again. She can't afford to take that long this time, so she's putting up walls and trying to cut ties as cleanly as she can. Just..." He paused and took a breath. "Just let her go, Josh. It's over."

I dropped onto the sofa and ran my hand through my hair. This was a nightmare. She was my best friend. How could I just pretend she didn't exist? Just act like my life wasn't a fucking disaster area with her gone? I didn't have the strength.

"I can't, Alex. I can't do that."

"Then you're gonna have to give her some time. Maybe she'll call you. We know that being cold isn't Carly's strong suit. I'm sure she'll come around soon."

"I guess I don't have any choice, do I?"

"No, honey," Alex confirmed. "You really don't."

Chapter 2

Summer 2003

I only spoke to Carly a few times that summer. Alex had told her how worried I was, so she called to let me know she was okay. She seemed distant, though. The minute I asked her about how she was doing, she'd change the subject to something clinical like work or the weather. She sounded tired all the time and, as Alejandro mentioned, she sometimes slurred her words as if she'd been drinking. My heart ached for her, but there wasn't much I could do.

I'd resigned myself to being on the west coast and if I was being totally honest, I didn't hate it. The weather was incredible, the lifestyle was fairly relaxed and I was starting to settle in. The only down side, other than being away from Carly, was my schedule. I was on set all day, every day. I'd been used to that during theater rehearsals, but production wasn't nearly as demanding. It took a lot to get used to. Aside from weekends, I didn't have a day off until we took a small hiatus in August. I tried convincing Carly to take some time off and come visit, but she refused, claiming deadlines and other weak excuses having to do with work.

Finally, at the end of July, she called me in tears, pouring out her heart. I suspected she had been drinking, but if it meant finally facing her emotions, I'd take it.

She had returned to her hometown for a class reunion with Alejandro and, from what he had told me, he'd been a little stern with her where I was concerned. Alex could be intimidating at times, but that worked to my benefit in cases like this. He'd pushed her into calling me and breaking down those walls she'd built.

I tried hard not to pressure her, but damn it, I wanted to see her! I wanted to show her how great California was. I wanted to go for a walk on the beach at sunset and give her a taste of the nightlife in Hollywood. I wanted her to help me find the perfect house to buy—not just for me, but for us. If I had my way, she'd live in it with me eventually and I needed her input. I didn't tell her that, of course, but it was definitely on my agenda.

"How are you?" I had asked her.

"Honestly?"

"Of course," was my immediate response. Did she really think I wanted her to lie? Besides, I already knew how awful she felt. It wasn't too far from how I felt myself.

"Horrible."

"Why, Coop?" I'd answered, using the nickname I'd started calling her almost the moment we met. "What's wrong?"

"I hate being here in our apartment without you," she'd said with a sniffle and I knew she'd been crying. "I hate that I can't stop thinking about you. I hate that I still love you. I hate that we're not together. It's affecting everything I *dooooo*." She sucked in a breath after a long sob. My heart was breaking. "I haven't written a decent article in three months. I sat outside the airport for almost an hour crying the day you left. I can't sleep worth a damn and I only lie on my side of the bed because part of me still wants you to be on your side. And I know I'm rambling, but if I don't get it all out now, I never will and I'll explode. Oh, and I wore my engagement ring to my class reunion because I didn't want Jason Metcalfe to hit on me and then I didn't want to take it off and I miss *youuuuu*!"

Chuckling to myself at Carly's outburst, I waited for her to catch her breath again before I spoke.

"Oh, beautiful . . . I've been waiting for this."

By the time our conversation was done, I had her convinced to at least check her schedule and consider a visit. I hoped she'd do it, but Carly was one of the most stubborn people I knew.

Sure enough, about a week before my hiatus, she called me and said she couldn't make it work. I wasn't surprised, but I was disappointed. However, since I was only slightly more stubborn than Carly was, I acted like it was no big deal. Instead, I talked about house hunting. I just didn't mention the part where I wanted her to be a part of the search.

I called Carly the following Sunday, still hoping that I could talk her into a visit. Unfortunately, my call went right to voice mail. That was typically what happened when she was avoiding me. It was obvious she was embarrassed by her outburst. I didn't need puppets and crayons to figure out what was going on: our ship had sailed and once again, we weren't on board at the same time. I waited and called again on Monday, but still got voice mail. I figured her friend Tisha would know what was going on, but since I didn't have her number, I decided to call Alejandro instead.

"Hey man," he said, cheerily answering the phone. "What's up?"

"Not much," I replied casually. "I just thought I'd give you a buzz. We haven't talked in a while."

"Josh, you never call me to just chat."

"Sure I do," I argued. "All the time."

Alejandro's laughter echoed through the phone.

"All right, fine." I admitted. "Have you talked to her?"

"Carly? No. Haven't you?"

"No. I haven't talked to her since last Tuesday," I told him.

"Tuesday? Are you sure?" Alex's voice sounded weird.

"Dude, I'm pretty sure I'd know if I had talked to her," I said. My impatience was obvious. "That's why I called you."

Alex mumbled something I couldn't understand.

"What?"

"Nothing," he replied. He seemed distracted. "Look, I've gotta go, but I'll call you back if I hear anything, okay?"

"Alex, I..." I began, but the line was already dead.

What the fuck?

I dialed Carly's cell again, as well as the house phone, but all the calls still went to voice mail. Her office gave me the same run-around they'd given me every time I called: she was *out.* I hung up and flopped down on the couch in frustration. I tried to call again the next morning with the same results and finally convinced myself that she just didn't want to talk to me. It was a bitter pill to swallow and one I wasn't sure I deserved, but there was nothing I could do. I threw my sneakers in my duffle, grabbed my iPod and headed to the gym.

I was leaving my realtor's office mid-morning on Wednesday when my phone rang. Glancing at the caller ID, I quickly answered with an ear-to-ear smile.

"Hey, stranger!"

"Hey," Carly said softly.

"Where have you been? I've tried calling you for days and it keeps going straight to voice mail. Alex told me he hadn't heard from you either and I got worried." I knew I probably sounded like an overprotective father, but she had me scared.

"I know. I'm sorry." She apologized, following it with a brief pause. "Long story short, I got hit by a car."

I nearly dropped the phone.

"What! Are you okay? Where are you? Are you hurt? Do you need me to fly out there? I can, you know."

"No, I'm fine. Really. I was crossing the street and some driver wasn't paying attention and clipped me."

She continued on, but all I needed to hear was that she was okay. It didn't, however, change the fact that my instincts told me to run to her side. I figured they always would.

"I miss you, beautiful."

I heard the catch in her breath.

"I miss you, too."

"Come see me," I pleaded. "You've got the time off, right? Get on a plane. Do your healing out here." Desperation wasn't one of my most appealing qualities, but I didn't care.

"Josh, we've been through this."

"It's a vacation, Coop."

"Josh..." Her voice was cautionary and I knew better than to keep badgering her.

"Fine," I surrendered. "I won't push you. Please just think about it."

Before she said goodbye, I heard her strangled sob. It was a sound that broke my heart.

I didn't know why she was resisting so much. It was obvious to me that we both missed each other and wanted to be together, so why couldn't she admit it? God, this was killing me . . . killing us both.

I talked to Carly a couple more times over the next month or so, but she kept the conversations brief and the focus on trivial things. She didn't bring up coming to LA and I didn't push it, either. If she wasn't willing to admit she still had feelings for me then I had to swallow my pride and move on, even if every fiber in my body was fighting me on it.

I won't lie: I debated taking a week off and flying to New York, despite Carly's claims that she was recovering just fine. Fate stepped in, though, and a bid I put in on a house was accepted by the seller. I got caught up in the process of home buying. Appointments with realtors, bankers and inspectors kept me busy through the next several weeks and the thought of going to New York was shelved for the time being.

Work kept me busy, too: between twelve-hour days at the studio, another three or four hours learning lines, and the time spent getting settled in the new place, I didn't have much time left in the day to do anything, much less pine away for a woman who didn't want me anymore. That part was both a blessing and a curse.

Despite being busy, every free moment I had was spent thinking of her. I thought about how her hair tickled my nose at night when she was curled against me. I would wake up in the middle of a dead sleep because I was sure I heard her voice whisper my name. I'd catch a glimpse of a curly-haired brunette passing me on the street and nearly wreck my car craning my neck to see if it was her. It was torture.

I only knew one person in Los Angeles who could help: Bobby Callahan.

My former bandmate was a clever bastard. He rarely got hung up on women. He treated them more like cars–when he got tired of driving one, he'd trade it in on a different model. If anybody could give me advice on how to get over Carly, I knew it'd be Bobby. I trusted him more than almost anyone.

We weren't always close, though. When the band had been together, we fought like brothers– and *not* those brothers who defended each other if anybody else picked on us. No, we'd been the brothers who were constantly at each other's throats regardless of who or what the cause was. We had our share of knock-down, drag-out fights. I'd sported bruises, a couple of fat lips and at least one black eye during our first tour. As we both matured, though, we grew out of it and settled into teasing and torment rather than beating the shit out of one another.

Bobby introduced me to my first lay. And my first shot of whiskey. And, though I'm not proud of it, my first line of coke. We'd partied pretty hard in those days. We both mellowed with time; he gave up the drugs long before I did, in fact. But since I'd moved to LA, we'd been in touch more often.

"Dude, you gotta just forget about her," he told me, with a shake of his head. He rested his elbows on the bar behind him as he observed the crowd in the club. I watched him as his eyes wandered up and down several female bodies walking by him.

"It's not that easy, man," I argued. "We were engaged! My family loved her. *I* loved her. I *still* love her." I shook my head knowing he'd never understand.

"That may be, but she's not here, dude," he said as he turned around, motioning to the bartender for another round. "It's time to move on."

Just then, a long-legged redhead saddled up next to me. She looked me over, flashed a too-perfect smile before turning to order herself a Cosmo. My gut told me to turn away. My dick, however, had other ideas, making me strike up a conversation with the woman before I could stop myself.

Bobby just chuckled, nudged me with his elbow, and gave me a nod as he stepped away.

The next morning, Red left without much fanfare. Thank God. I wasn't in the mood for small talk and with the hangover I had I didn't feel like being nice, either. I wasn't proud that I hadn't asked her out on an actual date, or even gotten her name, but perhaps the less I knew, the better.

As it turned out, pride was the least of my worries. I ended up going out with Bobby almost every weekend, repeating the "Red situation" more than once: never exchanged names, phone numbers or interests beyond what happened in bed. My heart was safer that way. Sadly, my liver wasn't.

There were numerous times when I woke in someone else's bed with very little recollection of how I got there. I would remember flashes of the night before that usually involved copious amounts of alcohol and flirting. Neither was independent of the other, of course. That wasn't my style. None of those women could ever be a replacement for Carly, though. The longer I went without speaking to her, the lonelier I felt, even though I was rarely alone.

Life had slowed down a little bit by late September and I'd whittled down my one-night stands to just once-in-a-while stands and mostly with the same girl.

I'd run into her at one of Bobby's notorious parties. Drinking at the bars had gotten too expensive, the crowds had become mundane, and with a new pool to christen, he'd decided the best idea would be to invite everybody to his place in Malibu instead. His house was teeming with people from

Friday night until Sunday afternoon when the last of the stragglers made their way to their cars.

Claiming the only empty stool at the makeshift patio bar, I set my empty glass down and waited for a refill. It had been a long week in the studio, and I wasn't much in the mood to socialize. Taking the fresh drink, I sat with my back to the crowd and took a swig.

"Don't I know you?" said a feminine voice from beside me.

I shrugged my shoulders, taking a quick glance at her as I swallowed my scotch, not meeting her eyes. "Um, I'm sorry, I don't know. I meet a lot of people." I turned a little in my seat, hoping she'd get the hint. I'd heard this come-on line for years and I wasn't falling for it this time, either.

"No, I do. I know you," she insisted. "You're Josh, right?"

Christ, here we go. I couldn't be rude. Not with ratings at stake. I took a deep breath, turned around again and painted on a smile.

"Yeah, I'm Josh," I said, my eyes lifting to meet hers. "And you're..."

Her green eyes shone back at me and familiarity punched me in the gut. God, I'd forgotten all about this beauty standing before me. "You're Abby Levy."

"You remember," she said, seeming pleased at my recall.

"As a matter of fact, I do," I said, my real smile replacing my fake one. I leaned forward and pecked her cheek. "God, how have you been?"

"I'm good. Yourself?"

"Better now." I said. And I genuinely meant it. I hadn't seen Abby since 1994, my first year in New York. Life had been kind to her. She still looked like the nineteen-year-old she'd been back then— like time hadn't existed in her world. Not a wrinkle. Not a gray hair. Not even a freckle from the sun. It was like she was airbrushed. I rarely used the term, but Abby was a goddess. A beautiful, blonde goddess.

"What are you doing in California?" I asked her.

"I was just going to ask you the same thing," she said with an ear-to-ear smile.

"Acting gig," I replied simply. "One of those roles I couldn't pass up, you know?"

Abby gave a slight snort.

Of course, she knew. Abby and I had shared one amazing night together back in the day, but before it could turn into anything serious, I called it off. I'd gotten an ass-chewing from my agent who was totally against actors having relationships . . . said they'd turn me soft and he didn't work with pussies. I gave my "I'm too busy for a relationship" speech to Abby, and while she hated it, she had no choice but to accept it. We remained flirty but left the sex at the door. Not that I had wanted to, though. It took a priest's resolve to walk away from her day after day, and I'd taken more than one cold shower after we'd spent time together. I suspected I'd be taking one that night, too.

"I got a contract with Ford Modeling a few years ago and decided in the summer of '95 that New York wasn't the place for me anymore, so they transferred me out here."

"So you've been in Cali all this time? That's great!"

"It's been good," she said. "I actually haven't done any modeling since my run with Vogue ended in 1999. But a couple years ago I started my own agency for models that weren't necessarily in their prime anymore."

"You're kidding!"

"No," she smiled proudly. "We had a huge influx of applications from women in their twenties whose jobs were being given to teenagers half their size. Believe it or not, women in this country don't really want to see fourteen-year-old girls modeling the clothes they see in *Redbook*. We've got a few hundred models signed and expect to double that by 2005."

I had no idea if that was a big number or a small one, but it was enough to impress me.

"That's incredible, Abby," I congratulated her. "Quite an accomplishment for someone your age."

"Thanks! I mean, who knew my experience would work in my favor," she reasoned. "Besides, my career being over was what inspired me to do it. I may have been aged out of the market, but I still had a lot to offer the industry so I founded *Belle Eros*."

There was no question about what she had to offer. At twenty-eight, she still barely looked old enough to drink. She was slim, but had slight curves in all the right places, and she was one of the few women who could stand barefoot and nearly look me in the eye. Her short skirt allowed me to take in her long, slender legs. They were just muscular enough to let me know she didn't miss a day in the gym. Her long, flaxen hair brushed my wrist when I put my hand at the small of her back. It was mostly straight, but curled up at the ends and reminded me of her personality–straight-laced for the most part, but just twisted enough to be fun. Her skin was an even, sun-kissed bronze and I knew without looking I wouldn't find tan lines anywhere. Her shoulders were strong, but she had that little dip on each side of her collar-bone to make her look feminine. Her adorable rosebud mouth reminded me of the dolls my sisters had played with when we were kids. She had a blush to her cheeks that made it so she didn't even need make-up. And her breasts. Good God, her breasts. I couldn't guess a cup size, but they were each easily a handful with plenty to spillover. I wanted to bury my face in her cleavage.

We left Bobby's not long after that and headed to a secluded spot on the beach. She slipped off her high-heeled sandals and carried them in one hand, the remainder of a bottle of Cabernet in the other. We took turns sipping the wine as we caught up on the last several years of each other's lives. Thirty minutes later and a half a mile down the beach, we finally stopped and rested on a wooden platform at the base of a cliff. I held her hand for balance as she lowered herself to a sitting position. I settled down beside her and we sat quietly listening to the tide crash against the rocks nearby.

Our silence was as comfortable as our conversation. Abby and I had always been good at both. It was what had made our friendship so easy all those years ago. It reminded me of Carly and how well we'd meshed that way, too. I broke the stillness and told Abby about her.

"And she just let you go? Called off your engagement and sent you here—just like that?"

I nodded solemnly.

"She's a fool," Abby said bluntly, punctuating her statement by finishing off the wine.

For the first time in months, I realized she was right. I rose silently, brushed the sand off my butt and held out my hand to Abby.

"What?"

"C'mon," I said. "Let's get outta here."

Sunbeams shone in narrow lines through the blinds across the floor in my bedroom and the only noise to be heard was the sound of Abby breathing rhythmically beside me. She was still asleep, her corn silk hair spread over my pillow. I propped my head on my hand and watched as she slept.

She was nothing like Carly and I appreciated that about her. Carly had been curvy and womanly. She had "a mother's body," as Ma had once said—full hips and an ample bosom. Mother's body or not, she looked normal to me. Some might call her average, but I always thought she was beautiful. She was shorter than I was: her head tucked perfectly under my chin. Her short legs had been more muscular than Abby's, though. Stronger, somehow. Carly's mane of coffee-colored curls barely reached her shoulders and seemed thicker than Abby's blonde locks. Even the color of Carly's skin was different from Abby's. It was more pale but freckled from years in the sun.

Everything about the two women was different, even the way they slept. Abby slept on her back with her long legs stretched out straight down from her hips, one toe peeking out from the sheets and pointing elegantly toward the wall opposite the bed. Her left arm extended above her head, her wrist limply hanging over her forehead. I asked her about it when she'd stayed at my apartment once. She said she always slept on her back so her eyes didn't get puffy by sleeping face-to-pillow. It also prevented sheet lines on her face, in case she had an early call or an audition. The shit you learned when you dated a model.

Carly had always slept snuggled close to me in the fetal position. Every inch of her would be covered with at least a sheet, regardless of how warm the temperature was in the room. Her face was always buried between pillows and my ribcage. She said she always felt safer with me there.

"Whatcha thinkin' about, handsome?" Abby's raspy voice whispered as she rolled to her side, facing me. The sheet slipped down her body and bared one rosy nipple to me.

"You," I said in response. Okay, so it was only half true, but if I had my way, she'd help it become fully true. I needed Abby in my life. I needed her to help me get my mind off Carly for good.

"Oh?" she practically purred. "Wanna be more specific?"

I smirked at her but didn't offer an answer. Instead, I leaned over her, covering her mouth with mine. Abby, ever in control, pushed at my chest, forcing me onto my back. Silently, she slipped one long leg over my hips and straddled me, her hair creating a curtain around our faces as we kissed. The muscles in my groin shot to life, and I pressed my hardness against the inside of her thighs. She let out a soft moan as she reached between us and stroked my length.

With a sleek, fluid motion, she slid her pelvis up enough for the head of my cock to snake between her slick folds and she eased it inside her. I couldn't hold back a groan as her heat enveloped me. Abby broke the kiss and snapped her body up, taking me deeper, gasping when her ass slapped against my balls. It was quickly followed by moaning as she began to grind against me.

Watching her face for encouragement, I drove into her slowly at first, then more quickly. I gripped her hips as we developed our rhythm. Her tits bobbed with every thrust and her mouth was frozen in a permanent "O." She raked her nails down my chest as she took charge and began bouncing her ass against my thighs. The room was filled with the sound of grunting, whimpering and moaning as we worked toward climax. Profane begging ensued on her part and I wasn't about to deny her the pleas she made so vocally. By now, I'd risen to a sitting position and had her long hair in my fists, driving into her in a rabid frenzy. She gripped my shoulders so hard, it felt like she'd drawn blood.

Abby reached orgasm first. As she threw her head back, her demands became more vulgar. Her filthy words were quickly replaced with heavy panting and then a silent stillness as the waves crashed through her. Her body quaking and clenching drove me to come, and I plunged into her once more, holding her against me as I emptied into her. Minutes later, with muscles finally relaxing, we fell into a sated tangle of arms and legs.

I kissed Abby's damp forehead and whispered, "Good morning."

She giggled and ran her finger down my chest before laying her head against it. Her breath passed over my skin like a warm breeze and I held her tightly. I'd missed this. And for the first time in ages, I didn't think about Carly.

Chapter 3

December 2003

Despite my relationship with Abby progressing, I was still haunted by the ghost of my ex-fiancée. I talked to Carly a few more times, but each phone call became a bit more stilted . . . every email, a little less personal. Although, according to Alejandro, my pride was smarting worse than my heart. I didn't know if he was right or not, but I didn't care. I just knew something had to be done. Abby was great *and* great for me. I needed to shit or get off the pot if this thing with her was going to work. I needed closure.

Abby had been so tolerant, so understanding. I owed her a clean break from my previous life in New York. For weeks after our first night together, I'd refused to leave the house once I got home from the studio. I blamed it on my schedule, but we both knew it was more than that. Depression had taken a tight hold of me and I could barely function, despite having every reason to be happy.

After dinner one night, she sat down on the couch, folding her legs under her as she propped her elbow on a pillow. She stared at me for a long time before speaking.

"Baby, I'm really getting worried about you."

I muted the television and clenched my jaw to keep my emotions from surfacing.

"You aren't sleeping well, you barely eat anything, you're drinking a lot, and the circles under your eyes are getting darker by the day." She listed off things I'd noticed myself but had refused to acknowledge out loud.

"Is it something wrong with me? With us?" I heard the quiver in her voice.

"Oh God, babe . . . no!" I picked up her hand and squeezed it tightly. "No, it's nothing to do with us. It's me. I just..." I drew a deep breath and let it out. "I'm just so fucked up."

She reached over, brushing my hair off my forehead and kissed my temple.

"Talk to me," she urged. "Whatever it is, we can work through it together."

"You wouldn't understand," I said, believing fully what I spoke. How could she understand that while I lay next to her every night, my thoughts go to a woman three thousand miles away?

"Try me."

I sat silently for what seemed like minutes, though I know it was only a few seconds and tears began to spill down my face. Abby deserved better than an ass like me.

"I can't do this anymore. You're right. This is about us. About you. God, you deserve so much better than this."

I heard the catch in her breath and I knew the panic in her body language as she pulled back from me, tucking her hands between her thighs in a protective stance. I'd been there and it fucking sucked. But I couldn't lead her on anymore. I couldn't do that to her. I inhaled deeply, manned up and wiped the tears from my face.

"I'm not good enough for you, Abs. You deserve someone who isn't broken . . . someone who can give you more than what you're getting, and I'm not him."

Abby bit her lip and let out a slow breath. "It's her, isn't it?"

I nodded.

She sat silent for a moment, then leaned over and ran her fingertip across the back of my hand. Softly, she spoke. "She isn't here. I am. That should tell you something."

"I can't be who you need me to be, Abby."

"You already are," she whispered. "You just need to believe it, too." Lacing her fingers in mine, she dropped to her knees in front of me and kissed the back of my hand. "I'm a patient woman, Josh. I love you and I'm not going anywhere."

It was then that I realized I was the one who didn't deserve her.

In a drunken stupor one night, I got the brilliant idea to send Carly a Christmas card in attempt for that sought-after closure. Abby had gone away for the weekend to visit a friend in Napa and I had entirely too much free time and, apparently, too many bottles of scotch in the house.

I'd already signed the rest of my Christmas cards the week before but the Glenfiddich in my system convinced me to use one of the remainders to let Carly know I was moving on without her. It would serve her right, after all.

I wrote out a long letter to her, pouring out my heart. I meant for it to be kind. I wanted to tell her how much I missed her, but how I knew this was for the best; two shots at trying to make it work showed that much. Unfortunately, my anger toward what could've been prevailed, and my temper got the best of me. I think I even referred to her as selfish and uncaring. Luckily for me, the booze kept me from sending that card. Instead, I ripped it in half and tossed it over my shoulder. The Shih Tzu I'd adopted a few weeks earlier immediately attacked it, chewing it into wet, slobbery shreds before I could stop him.

"Tango! Damn it!" I scolded as he took off down the hall in a black and white blur, pieces of the card still in his mouth. I grumbled to myself and sank back into the sofa, scrubbing my hand over my face and letting out a growl of frustration.

I was never one without words and it pissed me off that I couldn't send a simple Christmas card to Carly. It shouldn't be this fucking difficult. I picked up the pen and scrawled out a briefer note on the next card but crumpled that one up, too. Nothing was coming out right. Finally, I just let the foil signature of holiday wishes speak for me and stuffed the card in the envelope. It wasn't poetic and it certainly wasn't kind, but hopefully she would understand how hard it was for me to come up with what to say. Carly had always possessed a sixth sense about that kind of thing with me. I hoped she hadn't lost it. I wrote out her address on a post-it note and made a mental note to have my assistant add it to the pile of envelopes waiting to be printed. I knew this wouldn't provide the closure I needed, but it was better than nothing.

With a four-week hiatus on the schedule at Christmas, I decided to head home to Boston to visit my family. I'd debated on going alone, but at the last minute decided to invite Abby along. I felt we were at a point where it was time to introduce her to the relatives.

"Are you sure, Josh?" Abby asked. "I mean, we're still trying to work through this Carly thing. I'm just not sure if it's the best thing for me to meet your family yet."

"I'm sure," I said. "I really want to start creating new memories, and I want you to be a part of them."

Her green eyes lit up and her smile spread from ear to ear. "I'd like that, too."

I hadn't seen my parents since May shortly before my break-up with Carly, and Ma was really digging into me about coming home for a visit. I'd already missed their anniversary in November. It fell around Thanksgiving, so missing one usually meant missing the other. If I skipped another holiday, I was pretty sure they'd disown me.

"Joshua!" my mother greeted me with a hug and a kiss on each cheek. "Come in, come in! You're gonna let all the warm air out!" Typical Ma—always worrying about wasting money. She took my coat and hung it up before I could even kick off my shoes.

"You must be Abby," Ma said with a smile. I could tell it was forced and that made me nervous. My mother had never hidden her disappointment about my losing Carly, but I hoped she would at least have enough tact to give Abby a chance.

"It's nice to meet you, Mrs. McCarthy," Abby said, extending her hand to my mother. Ma looked down at her hand, over to me then back to Abby. Reluctantly she took it and gave it a weak shake.

"Please, call me Margaret." Ma was polite, but not the least bit warm toward my girlfriend. "Let me take that coat for you." She held her hand out as Abby slipped her cashmere coat from her shoulders and gave it to my mother who grabbed it roughly at first, then noticing my scowl, loosened her grip. I heard the smallest huff of judgment escape my mother's lips as she slipped it over a hanger and tucked it in the closet.

So much for tact. God, I hoped Abby didn't pick up on the chill in the room.

"Hey Pop," I said, greeting my father with a hug.

"Good to see you, son," he said with a firm pat on my back. "Abby, it's a pleasure to meet you. We've heard a lot about you." At least Pop seemed friendly as he gave her a quick hug. I relaxed a little. "How was the flight?"

"It was good," I said, attempting small talk. Abby had a smile, albeit painted-on, as she stood silently next to me. Yep, she'd picked up on Ma's cold shoulder. I knew it was going to be a long weekend.

"How long can you stay, Joshua?" Mom said, closing the coat closet behind her.

"For the love-a-God, woman! Let them unpack before you start sendin' them back off again, will ya?"

"Aww, quit runnin' your suck, Colin!" Ma smacked his arm. She was used to Pop's teasing after all these years together and their rhetoric was comforting to me. "Good Lord, Joshua, you're so thin. Don't you feed him, child?" She frowned at Abby before looking her over from top to bottom. "Cripes, you're not much better. Both of you come with me and let me fatten you up."

Without giving Abby a chance to reply, Ma practically yanked my arm out of my socket, pulling me to the kitchen. The fragrance of spices filled the air and I breathed in the familiar yeasty aroma of her homemade baguettes. We'd eaten during our layover in Chicago, but the delicious smell coming from the kitchen made me forget about the airport sandwich I'd had hours ago.

Ma pushed me into a chair at the table and my father followed us, Abby's hand tucked inside his elbow. She'd made a friend in Pop, and I was glad. At least somebody was trying to make her feel welcome. I made a mental note to talk to Ma after dinner. Abby didn't deserve such a cold welcome.

Pop pulled out a chair for Abby, which she promptly took. She gave an appreciative gaze at my father. He returned it with a wink and took his usual place at the head of the table. Ma had never let us men help with meal preparation. She always said it was her way of showing love. Guests were also excused from dinner duty, at least the first visit. After that, she considered them family and they, too, were expected to help.

She hurried in with a hot pad and a basket of freshly broken bread. Returning a moment later, she placed a giant pot of meaty stew on the pot holder and carefully dipped out steaming bowls of it for my father, Abby and me. As usual, she served herself last and before we dug in, my father said grace.

As we ate, Ma asked me questions about work and the new house, gave me her guilt spiel about missing Thanksgiving and their anniversary, and announced proudly that my brother Matt and his wife were expecting another baby. This, too, was her way of adding more guilt to my life.

"So we got a Christmas card from Carly the other day," Ma said nonchalantly, but the bread in my mouth dried up like a crouton the minute her name was mentioned. Abby's hand stopped mid-air as she brought a spoonful of stew to her mouth. I heard her softly clear her throat before she continued eating.

I tried not to react noticeably, but I could sense both my parents watching me out of the corners of their eyes for my reaction. I swallowed hard and took a sip of wine.

"Oh, yeah? What'd she have to say?" I asked politely after swallowing another bite.

"Oh, she didn't really say much," Ma replied, taking a small sip from her spoon. "Just wished us a Merry Christmas and hoped the card found us well. She promised to call after the first of the year."

"That's good." I said quietly. "I know how much she enjoyed her conversations with you."

"So, tell us, sweetheart," my father redirected the conversation after an awkward silence filled the room. "How did you and Josh meet?" He patted the back of Abby's hand, which was clenched in a fist around her napkin at the moment.

I sighed in relief when she let go of the napkin, smiled at my father, and proceeded to tell him about our days in New York and then the party at Bobby's where we reunited. Pop's well-directed questions led us through the rest of dinner and while Ma was quiet, I was grateful for her silence. With my mother, you never knew when her moxie would get the best of her, and she'd blurt out whatever thoughts were rattling around in her head.

"Joshua, help me with dessert?"

"Sure, Ma." I agreed and grabbed empty dishes as I followed her into the kitchen. I rinsed bowls and stacked them in the dishwasher as Ma sliced into a freshly baked pie. The silence between us was palpable and I knew it wouldn't take long before she'd snap.

She didn't disappoint. She dropped the knife with a clatter and braced her hands on the counter.

"Jesus, Mary, and Joseph, son! Why did you ever let Carly go? She was perfect for you. She kept you grounded. She kept you focused. And you blew it. You blew it!"

Nausea rolled in my gut and I reached for the dishtowel hanging on the fridge door to dry my hands. My mother wasn't known for her tact, but even this was beyond her usual scope of being opinionated.

"Ma," I began but was interrupted.

"Seriously, Joshua," she continued. "I'm sure Abby's a lovely girl, but there's a history here that she's not a part of. And she's barely muttered a single word all night. Is she too good for us?"

"Ma, this is so inappropriate," I argued, tossing the dishtowel on the counter. I glanced into the dining room to see if Abby or Pop had heard any of Ma's rant. The two were silent and Abby stared at the tablecloth in front of her with her hand fisted around her napkin again. Yep. They heard.

"Please stop."

She didn't.

"I want to know how you could give Carly up so easily. Women like her don't come around every day, you know." Her voice got louder as she went on. "You act like girls fall from the sky. That by getting rid of one, another one is just going to magically appear. I mean, sure, women come along every day–no offense to Abby–but not women like Carly. Carly was the best thing that ever happened to you." She finished with a huff and a long deep inhale.

"Ma, Carly let *me* go," I shot back in a shouted whisper. "It wasn't my choice. She doesn't want me. She made it clear when she packed my things and drove me to the airport. And did you even stop to think that maybe Abby's quiet because she's scared that you won't like her?"

Ma picked up the dishtowel and covered her mouth as she coughed. I wasn't certain, but I thought I saw her eyes glisten. If the woman was crying, that would put the clincher in my holiday.

"I'm sorry, son. I just..." She paused and cleared her throat again from behind the towel. "I just really thought you two were good for each other. I loved that girl like my own flesh and blood."

"I loved her too, Ma." I said quietly. "I loved her more than anything, but I can't dwell on things. She doesn't want to be with me. She wouldn't even come for a visit. What's done is done, though. I've moved on and I'm happy now, Ma. Abby's a wonderful woman and I love her."

She looked up and sure enough, unshed tears puddled in the corners of her eyes.

Shit.

"Did you ask her, son? Have you asked her to come see you?"

"Yes, Ma. I asked her many times and she refused." I knew my mother had always favored Carly, so this disappointment wasn't surprising. It just sucked to deal with it. I had enough of my own confused emotions without having to nurse my mother through this break-up, too. "I have to face facts, Ma: it's over between Carly and me. That's why Abby's here. I'm moving on and you need to, too."

My mother pursed her lips and finally gave a slow nod. "Fine. But, I don't have to like it." Her chin jutted up in one last defiant statement of bullheadedness.

"Margaret," my father cleared his throat from the doorway and spoke quietly, but firmly. "There's a young lady in the other room who deserves your apology." Pop never spoke a word of criticism to my mother, so I was a bit surprised by his reprimand.

For the first time in her life, my mother didn't say a word. She just nodded and returned to the dining room.

"Thanks, Pop."

He gave a head dip and picked up the knife Ma laid on the counter. He continued to dish up pie and when he felt they'd had enough time to talk, we returned to the table, dessert plates in hand. When I sat down, I reached over to squeeze Abby's knee. She jerked it away and refused to meet my gaze. God, what a mess this was. The worst part was that Ma had really made me reflect on things again. I thought I was past this point.

Thankfully, Carly's name wasn't mentioned again, but neither was anything else. In fact, nobody said much of anything through dessert, so my mind retreated to last Christmas when I'd announced my engagement. So much had changed between then and now. Carly was a ghost I wouldn't easily shake, though I knew I needed to. I got a knot in my gut as I thought about it more. There was only one way of ridding myself of her specter—I had to see her face-to-face.

Chapter 4

February 2004

My palms were sweaty and I could tell I was starting to pit out under my suit jacket, despite the frigid winter temperatures outside. I wondered if Sinatra ever dealt with pit stains when he was nervous. Yeah, like my idol was ever nervous.

I watched out the window at the snow-slicked streets as the chauffeur flew uptown toward our apartment. Well, Carly's apartment, I guess. It hadn't been *our* apartment in almost a year. Tonight would determine if it ever would be *ours* again. A couple glasses of scotch helped calm my nerves before I left the hotel, but it had worn off a while ago and my nerves were back in my throat again. The town car bounced slightly as it passed through intersections and I took a couple of deep breaths, scrubbing my hand over my face anxiously.

My cell phone buzzed in my coat pocket, but I didn't reach to answer it. I knew without looking it was Abby. She had called me no less than a half-dozen times since I arrived in New York City that morning. Things between us had been tough since the debacle at my parents' house at Christmas and, with good reason, she was feeling a little uneasy. She also was less than thrilled about my trip to New York.

"You didn't even defend me, Josh." The look on Abby's face was distant and cold, something I'd grown accustomed to these last few weeks. "And now you're going to New York to see her? I don't like it. I don't like any of this."

I tucked my shaving kit in the suitcase and went over to the side of the bed where Abby sat, her arms crossed like a defiant teenager.

"Baby, I know you've got concerns," I said, crouching down in front of her. "But don't you want this to be over with once and for all? So we can move on?" I searched her eyes for affirmation. She huffed instead.

"Besides, it's not like I'm staying at her place. It's one dinner. A few hours out of like, three days. The rest of the time, I'll be working. You know that. Are you so insecure that you can't give me one dinner with her?"

Her eyebrow lifted sharply and I thought for a moment she'd turned into Scarlett O'Hara with her stubborn chin jerking upward. "I'm not insecure, Joshua. I don't trust her. There's a difference."

Good Christ, with the splitting of hairs!

"Well, you don't have to trust her, you only have to trust me," I assured her, not letting my gaze leave hers until she gave in.

"Fine," she said, tone full of obstinance. *"Just don't make me regret it."*

I told Abby my visit was for closure, but I think down deep she knew me well enough to suspect it was more than that. Women always picked up on that kind of stuff—hence the incessant phone calls all day. It wasn't that I didn't care about Abby. I knew I did; I just didn't know how much. The falling out with my mother at Christmas forced me to say the L word out loud, but I wasn't sure if that was out of Abby's defense or if I actually felt it. The whole thing had me thrown for a loop. I just needed to get closure on my relationship with Carly before I could move on with a clear conscience. Now that I was here in our city—the place Carly and I had called home together—I couldn't help thinking that maybe closure isn't what I wanted at all.

The car pulled up in front of Carly's building and I glanced up at her windows. A light shone through her sheer curtains and I could imagine her flitting around as she got dressed. I used to love watching her get ready for an evening out. She had this little ritual she did after every shower that left the house smelling like a cross between vanilla and strawberries. I smiled involuntarily at the memory.

"Just stay here," I said to the driver as I leaned forward. "We'll just be a minute."

"No problem, sir," he said, glancing up at me in the rearview mirror.

I inhaled deeply and opened the door. Buttoning my jacket, I climbed the stairs to the front door and pushed the button for Carly's apartment. A small light came on above the top of the security panel and I heard a camera click on. Nice. I always thought the place needed better security.

"Hello?"

"Hey, Coop," I said, giving a slight wave at the camera. "It's me."

"C'mon up," she replied. "I'm almost ready." With that, the door buzzed and I pulled it open as the light turned off again. I made the familiar ascent to my old home and the knots in my stomach got tighter.

What the fuck, Josh? Relax!

I blew out a couple of breaths and knocked. Carly opened the door and I lost all sense of who I was. She was bewitching. Before I realized it, I had my arms wrapped around her and my nose buried in her hair.

Strawberries and vanilla. Some things never change.

Reluctantly, I let go and pulled back, holding on to her hands so I could take her in. I couldn't help letting my eyes wander over her from head to toe, absorbing every detail of her appearance. She'd let her dark brown curls grow out and the hairstyle she wore framed her face like a portrait. Her face looked more mature, though I wasn't sure how that was possible; it had been less than a year since I'd last seen her. She had the same beautiful blue eyes, slightly-upturned nose and perfect lips that curled up in a smile.

I lifted her hand above her head and spun her around. The skirt of her black dress swirled around her pale thighs and I couldn't help wanting to feel those thighs wrapped around me later in the night. My groin stiffened momentarily at the thought.

"Damn girl, you look good enough to eat!" I grinned at her and silently wished I could.

"Well, since I'm probably not on your snooty California diet, you'll have to settle for dinner," she teased.

Not if I have anything to say about it, I thought to myself. My phone buzzed in my breast pocket like a shock collar and I was reminded of the other woman in my life. I cleared my throat.

"You ready to go?"

She muttered a response, but my focus was on her back as she strolled toward the bedroom. As my gaze centered on the sway of her hips, I realized I'd made a huge mistake by coming here. This wasn't closure. This was fucking torture.

Carly set her empty glass on the table and waited for me to speak. I couldn't *not* tell her the truth. Not after all this time. I had to be honest.

Now or never, McCarthy. Spit it out.

I picked up her hands and ran my thumb over the backs of her knuckles. Her hands had always been home base for me–my calm and my constant came from holding her hands. I'd missed this.

"Carly, I met someone."

I held my breath as I awaited her response.

"I'm sorry," she said. "What did you say?"

She heard me just fine. I could tell by the lilt in her voice. I grinned slightly at her clever maneuver in making me repeat myself. She always claimed she didn't play games, but she knew what she was doing to me. I looked down at her hands, running my thumb up her forefinger and across her knuckles again.

"I said I met someone. Well, actually, I ran into an old friend a few months ago, and things clicked and..."

She jerked her hands away from mine so fast, my palms hit the table unexpectedly and I stopped mid-sentence. When my eyes met hers, I would have rather been dead. Her pupils narrowed and her lips pursed as she huffed out a breath. I was somewhat grateful the waiter hadn't brought her another drink because I'd probably have been wearing it by now. Fuck, the truth was overrated.

"I'm sorry. I'm sure it seems sudden," I said as I looked down at my hands and picked at my thumbnail. My breathing was shallow and I was waiting for her to explode any moment. When she finally opened her mouth again, it wasn't volcanic, but soft and kind–something of which I was totally undeserving.

"Congratulations. I wish you happiness."

I raised one eyebrow curiously. "You mean that?"

"She's a lucky girl," Carly said, almost in a whisper and I knew then she was just being polite. She was pissed as hell but she refused to cause a scene in public. I didn't blame her for being angry. I kind of hated myself at this point. Her smile said one thing, but I knew she didn't wish me happiness. She wished me death. Death and despair.

A few moments later, as she caught me up on her life, that despair struck like the venom of a poisonous snake. She told me she'd planned on visiting me in Los Angeles, as a surprise. She wanted to see me and had organized a trip.

"The night before I left for LA," she began, "I was assaulted in my apartment. The guy raped me, he stabbed me repeatedly, and he left me for dead."

Nausea rolled through me and I nearly lost what little I had in my stomach. I blinked several times. Surely this was a story she was making up. She was writing a book or relaying something she'd heard on the news. This couldn't have happened to Carly–*my* Carly. But I knew it had. It showed in her face.

"Oh Jesus, Coop," I muttered helplessly. I reached across the table to hold her hand, but she kept her arms wrapped tightly around herself. My chest ached in response.

"There's more."

More? I didn't know if I could take any more. The rage I felt toward the son of a bitch who violated her was overwhelming and my hands shook with fury. I gripped the tablecloth to keep from trembling.

"I was pregnant . . . with our child."

My heart stopped beating. I stared at Carly and I saw through the walls she'd put up in the time since I'd left. I saw the sweet, naïve girl I'd fallen in love with over ten years ago . . . the vulnerable, innocent spirit she'd carried so proudly. All that was gone now and before me sat the shell of a woman who'd been beaten, robbed of our baby and left for dead. Her hardness was apparent now and I realized that was what I noticed when I walked through the door of her apartment earlier in the evening. It wasn't maturity I'd seen; it was brokenness.

I wanted to tell her I would stay here with her now—that Abby meant nothing to me after all—that I would never let anything bad happen to her again. That I would protect her every moment for the rest of her life, but I couldn't form words. I couldn't even blink.

Carly spoke and I know I answered, but I couldn't tell you what I said. I conversed on autopilot, asking what I hoped were the right questions. Finally, I couldn't take being separated from her another moment and stood up. I took her hand and much to her objection I pulled her to her feet and led her to the dance floor.

I needed to hold her. I needed to show her somehow that I loved her, that I'd never stopped loving her, and that I couldn't live without her.

I wrapped my arm around her slender waist and placed my hand on her lower back, pulling her against me. I held her other hand against my heart as we danced. Her rigid body fought me at first, but I was relentless in my goal. She needed to know I was here for her now. She finally surrendered and I felt her body shape to mine.

When the song was over, I pinched my fingers across my eyes, wiping away evidence of my unshed tears. I threw a stack of twenties on our table and left our uneaten dinner there. I needed to be alone with Carly. If I couldn't tell her how much I needed her, then I would show her, damn it. We silently made our way back to her apartment and I followed her upstairs.

She stopped inside her doorway and put her hand against my chest, lowering her head under my chin and I hugged her against me, kissing the top of her head.

This was how it was meant to be: Me. Her. Always.

"The day I met you, I knew I would love you for a lifetime, Carly." My voice cracked and I cleared my throat to cover it up. "That hasn't changed."

Her posture tensed a bit and she pulled away, looking up at me. Her eyes were red and her cheeks were wet with fallen tears. She cupped my cheek in her hand and I leaned my head toward it.

"Everything's changed, Josh." Her mouth curled into a sardonic smile. "But it was supposed to. It's Abby's turn, now."

My knees buckled and I had to catch myself. *No! No! This isn't happening!*

She rose on her tiptoes and pressed her lips to mine.

"Goodbye, Josh."

Chapter 5

Goddamn it! How did this happen?

I stood outside her door for a minute, gripping the door jamb while I struggled to compose myself. The asshole in me wanted to beat down the door, take her in my arms and never let go, but obviously that wasn't an option. I finally shook myself out of it and slowly descended the stairs while pulling out my phone. Abby had called once more, but I ignored the voice mail icon blinking at me. I couldn't handle dealing with her right now.

I had to talk to Alejandro. If he'd known about this and didn't tell me I would never forgive him.

The phone rang twice before Alex's voice greeted me.

"So, how'd it go?" He knew my plans for tonight, and while he tried talking me out of coming, he seemed as curious as I was about how it would go.

"Did you know?" I ignored his greeting. "Did you fucking know?"

"Whoa! Did I know what?" his tone sharpened.

"Did you know about the attack? About the rape? About the baby? Did you fucking *know*?!" I screamed into the phone.

"Slow the fuck down, Josh." I heard the background noise go quiet and I knew he'd muted the TV. "What are you talking about? Who was raped? What baby?"

By now, I'd reached the car and jumped in the backseat, barely able to give the driver instructions on where to go.

"Josh, what the hell is going on?

"Tell me the truth, Alex," I said, with a voice steadier than how I really felt. "Did you know Carly was attacked last year?"

"She was what?" His surprise seemed genuine, but I wasn't sure.

"Carly was attacked last fall. That car accident she said she had? It was bullshit. She was raped. Did you know anything about it?" I knew my voice was accusatory, but I didn't care.

"Of course I didn't know. Jesus, Josh!" He was silent for a moment. "Rape? Seriously? Why didn't she tell us? And what about a baby?"

"She was pregnant, Alex. She was having my baby, but when she was attacked, she miscarried." My tone had lessened in its severity and I spoke more quietly now. "Did you hear me, man? She was carrying our child!"

"I heard you," Alex said simply.

"You swear you didn't know?"

"I swear to God, I had no idea," he replied. "Shit, man, I'm sorry."

"I gotta go," I said dismissively. "I'll talk to you later."

I clicked *END* and closed my phone. The streets were more deserted now. Melting snow streaked down the windows of the car as I stared at street lights and displays in darkened storefront windows. My anger and frustration at the situation finally hit me and I let go of the silent tears I'd been holding for the last hour. Heartbreak was bad enough, but I had no idea how to mourn this kind of loss.

My phone rang again and I glanced at the caller ID.

Abby.

I needed some time to myself, but knew if I didn't talk to her, I'd never get it. I answered the call.

"Hey," I said, trying to sound as normal as possible.

"Josh?" Abby's voice immediately expressed concern. "I've been trying to reach you for hours. Are you okay?"

I let out a long breath and pinched the bridge of my nose.

"Yeah, yeah," I answered. "I'm fine. I'm sorry I didn't call you when I landed. I've been busy since I got here and haven't had a…"

"No, no, no. It's okay. I was just worried." She sounded a little less tense now. "You're sure you're okay?"

"Yeah, I'm sure."

She was silent for a moment.

"Look, Abby," I took a deep breath. "Can I call you in the morning? It's been a long day."

"Umm . . . yeah," she paused and I knew her womanly radar was probably going off. "Yeah, I'll just talk to you tomorrow."

"Okay. Goodnight."

"Goodnight, Josh. I love you."

"You, too," I replied, feeling even more confused than ever as to whether or not I meant it. But I knew if I didn't respond in kind, it would start a debate that I didn't have the energy to fight at the moment.

I hung up and asked the driver to stop at a liquor store before returning me to the hotel. I'd learned to do most things sober over the years, but this was beyond normal expectations, even for the most balanced person and let's be honest, "balanced" has never been a word most people would use to describe me.

With a hangover jackhammering at my head in every direction, I rolled over with a groan. Light appeared through a sliver in the curtains, and I cursed its existence. Nausea churned through me and I raced to the bathroom in just enough time to empty what was left of the Glenfiddich in my system. Sweet Christ, what had I been thinking?

Carly.

Ahh yes, I remembered clearly. I sat up, leaning against the cold tile of the bathroom wall. Rest-ing my elbows on my knees, I propped my head in my hands and exhaled slowly as I thought about last night's conversation with Carly.

She'd made it abundantly clear that she'd moved on and somehow expected me to do the same, as if we'd never met. Her distance, emotionally, was hard for me to stomach at the time and continued to sit like a lead weight in my gut. More so was the recollection of the child she lost. *Our* child.

I scrubbed my hand over my face and carefully stood up. I rinsed my mouth out and looked at my reflection in the mirror. I was a fucking mess. My eyes were bloodshot and accompanied with bags so dark I looked like I'd gone a few rounds with Mike Tyson . . . and lost. I splashed some water on my face and returned to bed.

Picking up the phone, I called the only person who would feel as heartbroken as I did over this thing.

It rang twice before she picked up.

"Hello?"

"Hey, Ma."

"Joshua? Is that you, son?" She seemed surprised. "What's going on?"

"Well, I kind of have some bad news," I began, but paused as my voice broke. I took a slow deep breath before continuing. "I saw Carly last night, Ma."

"How is that bad news? You guys reconciled, right?" She seemed so hopeful and I hated disappointing her.

"No, Ma. We didn't reconcile. In fact, she made it clear she doesn't want to see me again. She told me something that happened and..." My voice waivered again. I cleared my throat and closed my eyes. "And I didn't know who to call but I have to talk to somebody. It shook me up pretty bad."

"You're scaring me, Joshua. What happened? Are you okay? Is Carly okay? Tell me!"

"Yeah, Ma. We're both okay. But, umm, last year Carly was in the hospital. She was attacked."

"Oh, dear Lord!" I could picture my mother clutching her throat and the color draining from her face. "But she's all right?"

"Yes, she's okay now, but it was so bad. She . . . she..." a sob caught in my throat and I pinched the tears out of my eyes. "She was pregnant with our child. And when she was attacked, she lost the baby."

My mother was silent.

"Ma, did you hear me?"

"Oh, Joshua," she cried. "Oh, my sweet boy. I'm so sorry. A baby? How is she doing now?"

"She seems to be all right. I mean, she's sad; I could tell that, but she looks good." I smiled at the memory of her in that silky black dress. "She's as breathtaking as she always was. She seems different, though. Older, I guess? But she's doing okay."

"And you, son?"

"I'm not so good. I can't believe she didn't tell me about the attack when it happened. It's like what we had never existed. I don't get it."

"Well, love, sometimes women can do strange things when something like this happens." My mother kicked into wisdom mode and I remembered why I called her. "Some girls are ashamed. Some are worried about being judged. Some think they must've done something to bring it on. Did she say why she didn't tell you?"

"She just said she didn't want me to come rushing back," I replied, explaining what Carly had said the night before. "She said she knew Los Angeles was where I needed to be and she didn't want me running back to New York to try and fix things that couldn't be fixed."

I heard her sigh on the other end of the phone.

"What? What are you thinking, Ma?"

"That she's right."

"You're hilarious, Ma."

"No, Joshua. I'm not kidding. She feels broken and she knows you're a fixer and that you'd give up everything that was important to you to try and take care of her. And son, you just can't fix that kind of broken. She knew you'd kill yourself trying."

"But I should've been given the choice," I argued.

"Perhaps," she replied. "But Carly had enough to worry about without having to take on guilt over what you'd be giving up if you came back."

"I can't believe you're siding with her, Ma!"

"Joshua Ryan, don't you raise your voice to me," she scolded. "And you know I love both you kids, but I understand Carly's reasoning and I can't pretend I don't. Not even to appease my youngest son with his bruised ego."

I huffed for a moment. She was right. This was more about my hurt feelings than it was about what Carly needed at the time.

"Ma, how is it that you're always right?"

"Oh, Joshua, I'm not always right. I just understand what a woman needs a little better than you do."

She was absolutely right about that. I'd never understand women as long as I lived.

"You said she made it pretty clear that things are over between you?"

"Yeah, I told her I'd always love her and nothing had changed, but she said it was Abby's turn now. And she kissed me goodbye."

Ma sighed again.

"Then you have to let her go, son."

This wasn't what I wanted to hear. My mother had always been the biggest proponent of my relationship with Carly, even at the expense of my current girlfriend. And to hear her give up on us too was almost more than I could handle.

"I mean it," she reiterated. "You told us at Christmas that it was time for you to move on and now you're acting like you didn't say any of it. You can't start seeing other women and expect Carly to agonize over you. It's time to move on. Carly said it's Abby's turn now and I agree with her."

"Ma, you can't be serious," I pleaded. "You always said Carly and I should be married."

"And I still believe that, but I also know you better than you realize and you're not in a place to give her what she needs right now. If you were, you'd have never gone to California in the first place, much less started something with this Abby girl. And from what we saw at Christmas, she seems like a decent match for you. You told me I needed to give Abby a chance. I am; you should, too."

I knew she was right and could do nothing but agree and say goodbye.

I stood at my hotel window overlooking Times Square and thought about Abby—how she looked in the morning when the sun peeked through the window casting rays of light across her blonde hair. I thought about how my body hummed to life when I'm around her. I thought about how she got my weird sense of humor, how she wasn't offended by my lame sexual innuendos, and how she didn't put up with any of my bullshit.

Carly had always been a bit on the naïve side, which was a total contrast from Abby. Abby had seen it all, done it all, and lived to tell about it. It wasn't that I didn't deeply care about them both, but it was for different reasons. Maybe Ma was right—it was time to leave Carly in the past and move on. Carly had been New York—she was an open hydrant on a hot summer day, an empty seat on a crowded subway and a comfortable blanket on a chilly afternoon. Abby was California: she was salt water and sand, sun-kissed skin and a convert- ible ride up the coast at dusk—everything I was now. I would never be New York again; those days were over.

Yes, it was time to move on. I picked up the phone and called Abby as I began throwing things in my suitcase.

Chapter 6

I lay next to Abby and ran my fingers up and down her bare spine. She'd met me at the airport when I got back to Los Angeles the night before, and without questions about what happened in New York she drove me home. She then proceeded to physically drain me of every ounce of the stress my body had acquired during the trip, most likely in an attempt to reclaim her territory. Hours later, we fell asleep in a sweaty tangle of body parts.

The sun gleamed through the blinds, illuminating streams of dust floating in the air like glitter. It made her long, blonde hair glow like a halo, and I couldn't help but compare her to Rapunzel. Her chest rose and fell with each breath and as if she could feel my stare, she shifted to her side, drawing one leg up toward her stomach. She let out a soft murmur and her lip twitched.

"Good morning, handsome" she mumbled as she opened one eye and looked up at me. Even without make-up, she was stunning.

"Morning," I replied as I kissed her forehead and wrapped my arms around her. I pulled her against me and nuzzled my face in the crook of her neck. "How'd you sleep?"

She stretched her legs out and yawned as her body returned to its curled-up state in my arms. "Like a baby. I always do when I'm with you."

Her words made me smile, but as the memories of New York came back to me, the smile faded and my body tensed. It didn't go unnoticed.

"Honey? Are you okay?" She looked up at me with concern in her eyes. "Something happened in New York, didn't it?"

My instincts were to just smile and shake my head, burying my feelings until I could process them, but something about the desperate way Abby searched my eyes made me decide to open up.

"Not really. Kinda—sorta—yes," I said. I drew a long breath and blew it out slowly. "I told you I was meeting Carly for dinner while I was in town."

"Our first fight. How could I forget?" she scoffed, then immediately appeared humbled. She propped her head on her hand. "Is . . . is there something I should be worried about?"

I immediately squeezed her hand and shook my head. "No, babe. You have nothing to worry about where Carly's concerned. It's over and has been for a while. She just told me something that kind of shook me up and I need to tell you about it."

"Okay," she said, with a hint of concern in her voice. She sat upright and pulled the sheet around her. "What's going on?"

From somewhere deep, I gathered the courage to tell her about Carly's attack and her miscarriage. Abby and I hadn't talked about kids or marriage—our relationship wasn't that far along yet—but she knew I had always wanted children. As I told her about the baby, her eyes became glossy, and she shook her head slowly, her expression full of sympathy.

"Oh, Josh," she finally said. "I am so sorry."

Not knowing what to say, I just nodded.

"You know, sometimes the universe has a way of working these things out," she said softly, placing her hand on my arm. "When the time is right, you'll be a dad. I know you will."

Abby didn't talk much that morning, but what she did say struck a chord with me that changed our relationship from casual to serious. She didn't jump into a jealous rage that I'd spent time with Carly, though after Ma's outburst at Christmas, she was damn sure entitled to one. She wasn't upset that I'd gotten Carly pregnant last year. She didn't accuse me of wanting Carly more than I wanted her. She just let me be and that was the greatest gift she could've given me.

Abby and I didn't bring up my trip to New York, again or the news I got when I was there, but

I thought about it often. I went through all of the typical stages of grief: anger, depression and denial. Fortunately, Abby would let my storms rage when they came and never condemned me for them. Unfortunately, my mourning penetrated my sleeping hours as well, and I spent several weeks either tossing and turning trying to get to sleep or tossing and turning trying to avoid it because of the nightmares that came when I did. It was a double-edged sword at times. I was damned if I did and damned if I didn't. And still, Abby was my rock through it all.

She'd been staying over quite a bit since my trip to New York and had even started keeping a few things at my house. We hadn't really talked about where our relationship was going, but I think we both knew it was getting more serious.

By the time filming for the season ended in April, she'd pretty much moved in. There were two months left on her lease, but other than furniture and a few boxes in storage, most of her stuff was at my house.

While I'd always been one to appreciate my solitude, having her there was a huge comfort to me. Idle time was hell on me, so just having another beating heart in the house helped break up the monotony.

That's not to say that Abby was my permanent shadow; if anything, she was quite the opposite, spending copious amounts of time at the office. She left shortly after dawn and rarely came home before the six o'clock news. I appreciated her work ethic and was proud of the independent woman she was.

Right from the start, she was adamant about splitting expenses. It wasn't a big deal to me, as I'd have the same bills whether she was there or not, but she was insistent about paying for her share. Each month, she'd write me out a check for her half of the mortgage, utilities and cable. The first couple months, I didn't cash them. I just tucked them away in my desk and figured I'd tear them up later. When she realized what I'd done, I caught all kinds of hell for it.

"Josh, why aren't you cashing the checks? That money is yours."

I met her tantrum with a chuckle.

"Don't you dare laugh at me, I'm serious," she argued. "I'm not some charity case you've taken in. I'm a competent woman, capable of taking care of myself, and I want to pay my own way. Furthermore, the last thing I want to do is to give your mother reason to think I'm some sort of gold digger."

"Abby, dear," I said, as I pulled her bullheaded body against mine. "Ma doesn't think you're a gold digger."

"Well, she doesn't like me. That's for sure."

"She'll learn to like you. I promise," I reassured her. "She won't have any choice. But as far as these checks go, they're wasted on me. I know you're capable of taking care of yourself, me and anybody else that comes along. There's no doubt about that. Paying half the bills doesn't determine that, though. It starts up here." I tapped her temple gently.

She growled in resigned frustration.

"Thank you," I replied, trying not to be smug.

By the time June rolled around, Abby and I had worked out most of the kinks of living together as a couple. I'd learned to compromise on decorating, and she'd learned that the big, ugly recliner wasn't going anywhere. Except maybe the man cave. Okay, so I compromised on that, too. The thing is I didn't mind compromising with Abby. I trusted her judgment implicitly and, if I really thought about it, that lamp *did* look ridiculous there. When I moved in, I put up a handful of pictures, set a few plants here and there and called it good. It was LA for Christ's sake. I didn't care what the inside of my house looked like. I spent ninety-percent of my time outside by the pool anyway, and Tango sure didn't give a damn if the upholstery from the couch matched the rugs as long as he could chew on both of them.

Abby had transformed the house into a showcase, though. She'd hired an interior designer (on her own dime, of course; God forbid, *I* pay for it). Together, they carefully redecorated each room, making the entire house flow like a well-crafted piece of art. All the walls had been painted neutral beige with white woodwork. The curtains and rugs blended with the pillows and furniture. I felt like I was living in a Pottery Barn catalog most of the time, but if it made Abby happy, that's what mattered.

And she was happy.

And the more I thought about it, so was I. For the first time since I'd moved to Los Angeles a year before, I felt content. The show had been a raging success and had just been renewed for two more seasons, along with my contract. My love life was back on track after my split with Carly. I had Abby to thank for that. Even my social life was improving. Abby and I spent quite a bit of time with Bobby and his girlfriend, Eve.

Eve was one of the models at *Belle Eros*, Abby's modeling agency, and when we introduced them, Bobby became smitten with her right away. Eve wore her red hair in long, full waves that reminded me of *The Little Mermaid*. She possessed the stereotypical fiery personality that redheads are known for. She had just enough sass to keep Bobby on his toes. He'd always been one to be in control of any relationship but with Eve, he was completely complacent. I was sure her long legs and big breasts helped with that. I teased him about it every chance I got. It wasn't often that I'd seen him hooked on just one woman, after all.

"She's the one, man," he told me one afternoon when the four of us were hanging out at his house. The ladies were sitting in the hot tub, absorbed in conversation that I didn't care to listen to. Bobby and I sat in matching Adirondack chairs, soaking up the rays while we cracked open a couple of Heinekens and emptied half a bag of pretzels.

"What? Man, you've known her all of like two months," I questioned. "What makes you think she's the one?"

"It's technically been three months, and I just know," he said. "Do you realize I haven't had any strange pussy since the night I met Eve?"

"You're a fuckin' liar. There's no way you haven't had at least one one-night stand in three months. Hell, you're more likely to have had three one-night-stands in one night!" I teased him unmercifully.

"Nope," he said with a straight face. "I haven't slept with anybody but her since St. Paddy's Day."

I remembered the girl he slept with that night, but as drunk as he was, I was surprised *Bobby* did. In fact, he was still hung over the next afternoon at the charity event for *Belle Eros*, where Abby introduced him to Eve.

Bobby's eyes shifted from me over my shoulder to his spunky other half. My eyes followed his, but instead of looking at Eve, I watched Abby. She was oblivious to my gaze. I could tell even from this distance that behind her sunglasses, her eyes were focused on Eve and she was in a whole different place. She brought her hand up once to wipe away an errant droplet of water, but otherwise she sat there listening to her friend, bubbles gurgling around her.

It was then that I began to think maybe Bobby wasn't the only guy to have found *the one*.

"Do you ever think about the future?" I asked Abby one evening as we were lounging around watching television. I'd been tossing the subject around in my head for days and had lost sleep as I tried to figure out where we stood, relationship-wise. I'd finally gathered the courage to ask her, spewing the words forward like vocal vomit.

"Hmm?" she replied, her eyes not leaving the TV.

"The future," I repeated, grateful that she didn't notice my anxiety-laden tone of voice. "Do you ever think about it?"

Her eyes glanced from the TV over to me, scrunching up her forehead in a confused expression. "What do you mean, Josh?"

"I dunno," I answered. "Us. Marriage. Kids. You know—the future. What are your thoughts?"

"Where's this coming from?" She reached for the remote and turned down *CSI*, looking at me.

I shrugged noncommittally.

"Well, something had to have brought it up," she insisted. "What's going on, honey?"

I got up, strolled over to the wet bar, and poured myself a small glass of Glenfiddich. I swallowed a large gulp before I turned around and walked toward her. Her eyes didn't leave mine as she waited for an answer.

I sat down on the footstool in front of her, setting my glass on the coffee table beside us. "I think Bobby's going to propose to Eve."

Abby gave a slight snort and a giggle. "Is that what this is about?"

"Yeah, I guess so. I just," I paused and began to gnaw at my thumbnail, as I tried to figure out what I wanted to say. Truth be told, I didn't have the first clue what I wanted to get off my chest. I paused, pretending to concentrate on my hands. "I just look at Bobby's history and can't believe he's actually settling down."

"Well," she said, "He's in love. That's what people do, babe. They settle down and get married when they're in love."

The muted volume on the TV was the only distraction in the room as we sat there for a moment.

"Are we in love?" I asked her, finally meeting her gaze.

She reached over and took my hands, lacing her fingers with mine. "I can't speak for you, but I am. I thought you knew that."

The corner of my mouth curled up in a slight smile and I nodded. "Yeah, I guess I know it. We just haven't really talked about it . . . haven't really said those words."

"What . . . 'I love you?'" she asked, tilting her head to the side slightly. "We say it every day."

"No, I know that. I mean, we haven't talked about being *in* love . . . what all it means to be that way."

"God, Josh, you're acting like such a girl," she teased.

The corner of my mouth lifted briefly in a grin, but my serious expression returned almost immediately.

"Okaaaay," she replied, still curiously searching my face for the point of this conversation. "What does it mean, exactly?"

"What you said."

"About Bobby and Eve?"

"Yeah," I nodded. "Settling down and getting married, having kids, that kind of thing."

"Josh, are you proposing to me?"

Was I? I concentrated on my hands again.

Was I really asking Abby to marry me? We'd been together less than a year. Was marriage the best thing for us? I mean, it probably was the next logical step after moving in together, but were we ready for it? What about kids? How many did she want? Did she want *any*? What would our parents say? Our friends? What about our careers? Would she still insist on separate bank accounts? Should we sign a pre-nup? There was so much still to discuss before jumping into something as serious as marriage.

"Josh?"

I jerked my head up, meeting her eyes again. "Yes?"

"Are you proposing?"

"Yeah," I said with a nervous chuckle, dismissing every worry with a shake of my head. I was certain my brain rattled like a sack of rocks. "I think I am."

"Then I think I'm saying yes," she met my laughter with a giggle of her own and I knew in my spontaneity I'd made the right choice. Abby had agreed to be my wife. I tackled her and we rolled to the floor in a storm of kisses.

Chapter 7

"We're thinking daffodil and charcoal for our colors," I overheard Abby say as she brought Phillip up to speed. She'd hired the wedding coordinator the week before. I had to chuckle to myself as *we* weren't thinking anything. I'd given Abby *carte blanche* where the wedding was concerned. She even picked out her own engagement ring—a high-carat diamond solitaire that was supposedly made of platinum, though you couldn't see the band for all the gemstones that encrusted it. She even argued about the cost of it, but I ended the argument by handing the jeweler my black AmEx. I was surprised I didn't have to fight her about who was paying for the wedding, but her parents settled that one, insisting on footing the bill for everything. Apparently, the only person more stubborn than Abby was her father, who came from a long line of frugal, hardworking men: hardworking, if you consider watching well-invested stocks pad your bank account, that is.

The thought of planning another wedding exhausted me after having spent so much time on the wedding with Carly. If Abby's parents wanted to pay for this and she wanted to handle all the details, I wasn't about to stop her. My role was to show up the day of the wedding and say "I do." I was okay with that.

Abby let out a shriek and I jumped in surprise.

"You are *kidding*!" Her eyes got big as saucers and her gestures became wildly animated. "How is that even possible, Phillip? The Plaza has a three-year waiting list!"

We hadn't set a date yet and as far as I was concerned, that was okay by me. We still had a lot to talk about and I wasn't in any hurry to rush down the aisle. I assumed Abby wasn't either.

I assumed wrong.

"September eighteenth!" she said as she hung up the phone.

The bottom dropped out of my stomach. That was just a little less than three months away.

"Next year?" I asked hopefully.

"No, silly! This year!" She said, smacking my shoulder lightly with the back of her hand. "There's apparently been a cancellation at the Plaza, and Phillip swooped in and booked it. Oh, I've always dreamed of getting married at the Plaza. I blame all the *Eloise* books my mother read to me as a child. I remember..." She became dreamy-eyed as she relayed her childhood anecdotes. I, on the other hand, tuned her out as panic seized in my chest.

What the fuck was she thinking? Two-and-a-half months? And in New York? Sweet Christ, why hadn't I paid more attention to her when she rambled on about wedding stuff? I'd have much rather had a destination wedding somewhere tropical or even at a vineyard in Napa. Anything *but* New York!

I was sure my eyes glazed over as Abby continued her reminiscence about the wedding she always dreamed of. In the meantime, I was too busy wondering how I could talk her out of New York. The thought of going back there made me nauseous. The Plaza was literally down the street and around the corner from Carly's apartment. Too close, if you asked me.

"...eymoon in the Maldives. What do you think?"

"Sure, sure. Sounds great, babe" I muttered, still zoned.

"Josh, are you okay?"

"Huh? Yeah, of course," I replied by rote. Realizing she was still staring at me with one eyebrow raised, I managed a smile and gave her a quick kiss. "I'm fine, babe. Just trying to figure out how we're going to plan such a huge affair in such a small amount of time. That's all."

"Oh, honey, I could pull this off in my sleep. Don't you worry about a thing." Her face beamed and I knew if anybody could make it happen, she could. Abby was the best when it came to pulling things together last minute. She'd told me story after story about how she'd always been in charge of fundraisers for her high school social commit-tee, planned all her sorority house events, and even arranged a surprise birthday party for her fa-ther while sick in bed with mono. That didn't even touch on the events she organized for *Belle Eros* as she worked to get the agency off the ground.

"Joshua, are you absolutely sure about this?" My mother's voice was filled with concern and while it would've been easy to tell her I wasn't sure, I knew it wouldn't do any good for her to continue worrying about this.

"Yes, Ma. I'm sure," I confirmed. "Abby and her mom have everything under control. Besides, she found some ridiculously demanding wedding coordinator who has already booked the venue, car service and a bank of rooms at the hotel. The dude seems to be able to get us everything we need de-spite the short notice."

I was met with a long sigh and I could picture my mother on the other end of the line with the phone cord wrapped around her finger, clutching and unclutching a wadded up Kleenex.

"Joshua, she's not..." her voice got lower. "She's not in *trouble*, is she, son?"

Shit, I wished. Okay, maybe not really, but it would've gone a long way in helping me feel more comfortable discussing the subject of children with Abby.

"No, Ma. She's not pregnant."

"Okay," she exhaled in relief. "I know it's the new millennium and all, but you know how we Catholics feel about that sort of thing."

I didn't remind her that Carly had been *in trouble* just under a year ago and she hadn't said a word about the sin and repentance involved in that.

"Yes, Ma. I know," I replied. "Abby isn't pregnant. I promise."

Coming in from the kitchen, catching the last few words of the conversation, Abby raised her eyebrows so high I thought they'd touch her hairline. I just rolled my eyes and waved my hand dismissively.

"All right, son," my mother said. "I'll get Abby's mother a list of addresses for our family and friends, by this weekend. I still think it's an awfully big rush, but I suppose you kids know what you're doing." Her repeated sighing contradicted her words, but again, I didn't feel like arguing with the woman. I didn't feel like arguing with any woman at this point.

When I hung up the phone, I pinched the bridge of my nose and blew out a breath.

"Your mother thinks I'm pregnant?" Abby blurted out. The look on her face was one of incredulity, and I didn't blame her. "She thinks the only reason you'd marry me is because I was knocked up with your illegitimate child?"

"Babe, she's just worried about the time frame is all," I tried to reassure her. "I promise, it's nothing personal."

"Your mother hates me."

"My mother doesn't hate you."

I was met with a huff and a scowl. Nursing Abby's tattered ego was the last thing I wanted to deal with, but I pulled her into my arms and kissed her up and down her neck, offering whispered words of reassurance. Her stubbornness and hurt pride finally relented a few moments later and she was once again on the phone, this time calling her mom to discuss wedding plans. I picked up my car keys, hollered that I was going to Bobby's, and before waiting for an answer, I left.

An hour later, I was sucking back a beer and shooting pool with Bobby. He had guys' night at his place once a week, but since meeting Abby, I hadn't been to too many: she thought they were childish. If I really considered that we didn't do much but play video games and shoot pool, it was kind of a waste of time. But with all the wedding talk going on, I needed the reprieve.

"Don't talk to me about your wedding, dude," Bobby said as he sunk the solid yellow ball in the corner pocket. "I'm still bitter about that best man thing."

I'd asked my brother, Matt to stand up with me, and apparently Bobby was still a little sour at being overlooked.

"I know, I know. I suck as a friend," I agreed. "But seriously, man. She's killing me with this shit. I know I'm not footing the bill for all this, but it's unbelievable how much she's spent so far. Do you know that the cake alone—not the groom's cake, whatever the fuck *that* is, and the bridal shower cake, we're talking *just* the wedding cake—costs over three grand?"

Bobby dropped his stick.

"Are you shitting me?" He looked at me with his bottom jaw somewhere near his knees. "It's sugar and flour, man!"

"Tell me about it! It's something like twelve bucks a slice and there are at least three hundred people on the guest list," I lamented. "It's insane. This whole thing has gotten completely out of hand."

"So rein her in."

I snorted. "Yeah, because reining Abby in is easy. Besides, this is all your fault, asshole." I gave him a death glare before taking my shot.

"My fault? What the fuck did I do?" He propped up his pool stick and leaned on it.

"You and your talk of Eve being *the one* and all that. And you haven't even proposed to her yet!" I gave my stick a shove and scratched, sending the cue ball into a side pocket. Growling, I yanked my beer off the bar behind me and took a swig.

Bobby laughed and placed the cue ball behind the head string, lining up his mark.

"Laugh all you want, man. I'm in misery here."

He sunk the six-ball swiftly and stood up, giving his attention to me.

"Josh, you're a pussy," he said. "If it bugs you that much, put your foot down. If not, then quit bitching, and let her do what she wants."

I gritted my teeth, exhaled loudly and watched him pocket the three.

"Eight-ball, corner pocket" he called just before shooting it home with a smug grin.

I tossed my stick on the felt, picked up my beer, and walked out the sliding door to the deck. The ocean crashed below and the sun cast an orange glimmer across the water as it lowered into the horizon.

Bobby joined me a moment later with two fresh beers. We stood elbow to elbow at the railing of his deck, sipping our Coronas and watching a flock of gulls dive-bomb a school of fish circling just beneath the surface of the water.

"Man, if you're this uneasy about the wedding, how do you really feel about the idea of marriage?" Bobby was nothing if not candid in his conversations.

"I dunno."

"You better know," he advised. "Before you make vows, you damn well better know."

"I guess it's all just moving so fast. I mean, a month ago, we weren't even talking about marriage, now we're picking out china patterns and drapes for the den."

"No," Bobby corrected. "*She* is picking out china patterns and drapes for the den. It's your house, too, man. You should get a say in stuff."

"Thing is, I don't really care. It's just dishes and fabric," I explained. "It's important to her, not me. I couldn't care less if we eat on china or Chinet. And I don't give two shits what color my curtains are. It's what happens *inside* the house that matters to me: the family and friends who visit us, the children we have, our lives together. That's what counts."

"And you guys are on the same page with that stuff?" he asked. "You know, kids, careers, families—all that stuff needs to be discussed before you guys walk down the aisle. Trust me. You don't wanna be arguing about the same shit ten years from now. Ask my parents."

Bobby's parents had six kids and, after their divorce, his father remarried twice more, adding another four half-siblings to their brood. His mother remained single and bitter, for which I didn't blame her. Bobby's dad was a hard man with a mean mouth, at times.

"I guess you're right," I agreed. "It's just the thought that we may have different ideals or goals in life at this stage of the game scares the shit outta me. I mean, what if we find out now we're not as compatible as we thought we were?"

"Then you call it off before it costs you half of everything you fuckin' own, man," he said, clapping me on the back and returning inside.

I watched as the very last sliver of sunlight dipped into the ocean and finished my beer. Bobby was right. I couldn't let things continue without making sure Abby and I were on the same page as far as our future went. It was a discussion we should have had before I ever proposed to her, half-assed as it was.

"Hey, honey. You're back early," Abby said, looking up from her notebook as I came in from outside. I'd affectionately nicknamed the notebook her *Wedding Bible*, as it held all the intricate details of our upcoming nuptials. "How's Bobby?"

"He's all right," I answered, trying to muster up some courage. I started to tell her that he'd invited us over for dinner the following night, but she was already scrawling something else into the Bible.

"Okay, so the cake has been ordered, and the caterer, florist and DJ have been booked. I hope you like raspberry filling, lamb, gardenias, and top-forty hits, by the way." She winked at me then continued. "The invitations are at the printer's as we speak. You need to go next week and get measured for your tux alterations, and I was able to squeeze in an appointment for my dress fitting tomorrow." She jotted checkmarks next to each thing on the list then looked up at me. "Can you think of anything we're forgetting?"

"Why are you asking me?" I questioned with a snort. "I thought Phillip was supposed to be handling all of this?"

"Well, he is, but I'm trying to double-up and make sure we aren't forgetting anyth—oooh! Bridesmaids' gifts!" she interrupted herself and scribbled in her notebook.

"We're already paying for their dresses," I lamented. "Isn't that enough of a gift?" Abby ignored me. At almost six-hundred bucks a dress, it seemed like a suitable-enough gift to me. It wasn't that I was a tightwad—hell, it wasn't even my money—but I detested unnecessary extravagance of any kind. Ostentation wasn't my thing. It never had been. And this wedding was turning into one hell of a diamond-encrusted, silk-tented circus.

"Oh! The rehearsal dinner! I almost forgot about that," she said, distracting me from my thoughts. "Do you think you could call your mom about . . . oh, never mind. I'll call her after dinner. It'll be easier if I talk to her, as much as I despise the idea."

I ignored her veiled insult.

"Babe, don't you think this is getting a bit out of hand?"

"Josh," she grumbled. "We've been through this already."

"I know, I know. A girl dreams of her wedding day from the time she's a little girl. Blah, blah, blah. I get it." I threw my hands in the air. "But seriously, Abby, how big of a deal does this thing have to be? There are only two of us here, you know."

"Blah, blah, blah?" Her green eyes got wide and she blinked rapidly several times as she took off her glasses and threw them on the table in front of her. She sat with her eyebrows arched nearly to her hairline, a piercing stare of outrage cutting through me.

"Look, that's not what I..."

"Blah. Blah. BLAH?"

Aww, Christ.

Abby seethed with anger and wounded vanity. I could tell from the bulging vein on her neck and the deep shade of red her face had turned.

"Babe," I tried to soothe her. "I didn't mean that." I took her hands and pulled her to the couch.

"Then what *did* you mean, Josh?"

"It's just that we're spending so much time and energy worrying about the details of our wedding that I think we're missing the bigger picture."

"What's that supposed to mean?" Her tone of voice was still pithy. "Isn't our wedding important?"

"Yes," I replied. "But not as important as our marriage."

Her eyebrows narrowed in a tight crease and she pursed her lips.

"Abby, how many kids do I want?" This wasn't how this conversation was supposed to go, but it was out there now, and I couldn't take it back.

"What? Why are you...? What does this have to do with..." she sputtered as I caught her off-guard. "Well, w-w-we need to wait a while before we have kids."

"You didn't answer my question," I stated, my voice exceedingly calmer than I felt.

"Well, I don't see how it matters right now. We aren't even married yet." Her voice was shaky, something I wasn't used to witnessing. Abby was always poignant, composed and profound with her thoughts.

"How many kids, Abby?" I repeated.

"Well, I suppose I could have one or two, but not right now. Maybe several years down the line. There's still a lot going on with building *Belle Eros* and it needs my entire focus for the time being."

I stood and shoved my hands into my pockets. "What?"

I just shook my head with an acerbic smile.

"No," she fired back. "You wanted this discussion. Don't back down now."

"You didn't listen to the question, Abby." I turned around in time to catch the sneer on her face before it disappeared.

"I most certainly did," she argued, jumping to her feet and propping her hands on her hips indignantly. "I heard everything you said."

"You may have heard me, but you didn't listen."

"Josh, can we quit playing word games and get down to what your problem is? I have things to do." She crossed her arms and shifted her weight to one hip, tapping her foot impatiently.

"*My problem*," I said, enunciating everything painfully slowly, "is that I didn't ask you how many children *you* wanted. I didn't ask about the when or the how or even the why. I asked you how many kids *I* wanted."

She jerked her stubborn Scarlett O'Hara chin and pursed her lips again, looking now at a suddenly intriguing piece of the rug.

I stepped closer to her and lowered my voice to barely a whisper.

"But you gave me all the answer I needed." I waited for her eyes to meet mine again before I continued. "You've been so focused on this wedding that you've forgotten there's a forever behind it–things that matter more in the long run than which fucking font is used on the invitations."

I noticed the clench in her jaw and the slight huff of her breath as she inhaled sharply in surprise.

"When you're ready to talk about the big stuff, lemme know." I held her gaze for a moment before spinning on my heel and walking upstairs, shutting the bedroom door with a firm bang behind me.

Chapter 8

We went to bed that night without saying a word to one another and she was gone in the morning before I woke up. I stewed about our argument all day. I'd been silent too long about a lot of things—the wedding was the least of them. My heart had been numb for so long before meeting Abby that, as a result, I barely remembered how to speak my mind. I guess I was afraid of her leaving.

Fucking coward.

That's what I was. I didn't know when I'd turned into such a pussy, but it couldn't continue, especially if Abby and I were to be married. She was a strong-willed, independent woman. That much was true. But she needed to learn that I wasn't a pushover, either. Up until that moment, that's exactly what I'd been. I might as well have worn a dress for as much of a man as I'd been the last few months. Shit had to change.

I checked my phone all day long between run-throughs. We broke for dinner around seven. Still nothing. By the time I left the studio at midnight, I still hadn't heard a peep from her. I turned left out of the lot and took the long way home, through Santa Barbara, up the coast to Malibu and back through the canyons that spotted the northern side of West Hollywood. It gave me the time to think about what I wanted to do.

Given that this was the first time I'd really stood up to Abby, her attitude seemed a little melodramatic. It wasn't like I told her to cancel the wedding altogether, for Christ's sake. I just wanted her to reel it in a little bit. And I certainly wasn't asking her to go off her birth control tomorrow so she could get pregnant on our wedding night. Jesus, I didn't want kids that soon, myself. But if this little silent treatment routine she was giving me was any indication as to what disagreements would be like during our marriage, I was starting to rethink that Harry Winston on her hand.

I pulled into the driveway and opened the garage door. Parked in its normal spot was Abby's Mercedes.

Thank God.

I turned off the car and punched the button to close the garage as I went into the house. I could hear a rerun of *ER* coming from the den and headed that way. Abby barely looked up as I entered the room. She'd already changed clothes and taken off her make-up. Sporting a tank top and pajama shorts, she was ready for bed. Her hair was piled on top of her head in a loose bun and the faint scent of her face wash hung in the air. She glanced over at me and drew a breath. She turned off the television and tossed the remote on the coffee table in front of her.

"Am I really that much of a tyrant, Josh?"

The meek, insecure voice that spoke wasn't like Abby at all, and for a moment, my instinct to downplay the situation pulled at me, but I knew that wasn't going to do either of us any good.

"Meh," I shrugged with the kindest agreement I could muster.

"That's not really the answer I was hoping for."

"What do you want me to say, Abby?" I threw my hands in the air. "I can't win here."

"Well, I don't want you to think I'm bulldozing you into anything," she replied. "Your mother certainly hinted at that fact."

"My mother hints at a lot of things. That doesn't make it fact."

"No," Abby said, picking at the fringe on a couch pillow. "But I know you respect her opinion."

"You're right. I do."

"And she has very specific opinions about me," she said, looking up with tears in her eyes. "And about Carly."

I nodded, picking at a hangnail on my thumb. I'd never seen Abby cry and I didn't want to see it now.

"Josh, I'm never gonna be Carly."

"I know that."

"I know you know, but can you please let your mother know?"

"She already knows."

"Sure doesn't feel like it," she lamented. "You should've heard the way she talked to me about the rehearsal dinner when I called her. It was like I was the wedding planner instead of her future daughter-in-law. She was so cold."

"You just have to give her some time, honey," I said, though I knew she'd probably never warm up to Abby the way she had Carly. Even though Ma agreed with my decision to marry Abby, it wasn't because she thought we were meant for each other; she knew I couldn't give Carly what she needed. But what about me? What about what I needed?

"We've been together more than six months, Josh. How much time does she need?" Abby brushed her cheek with the back of her hand and wiped it on her shorts.

"I don't know." I reached over without looking at her face and took her hand in mine, giving it a squeeze. She gripped my hand and I got a glimpse of how vulnerable she was underneath her brave façade. "But it doesn't matter. You're going to be my wife and the mother of my children. That's what counts."

Abby tensed up a little bit and loosened her grip on my fingers.

"You will be the mother of my children, won't you?"

She licked her bottom lip before sucking it between her teeth and biting down.

"Abby?"

"Someday," she finally said.

"Someday, meaning...?" I drew out the question. "A year? Five years? Ten? What are we talking here?"

"I don't know," she said noncommittally, as if I'd asked her what she wanted for dinner.

"Well, I need to know." I let go of her hand.

"Josh, I can't give you a date," she answered, folding her arms and stuffing her hands under her elbows. "I've got a lot of work coming up, not just for the agency, but for my own portfolio, too. I'm not ready to model maternity clothes just yet."

I looked at her for the longest time before speaking.

"Fine," I replied in surrender. "But you are willing to have children with me, aren't you?"

"Yes. Just not right now." Abby ran her fingertips over my arm and smiled. "I want children, Josh. I do. I just don't know how many I want or when I want them."

"Fair enough," I said, picking up her hand and kissing her fingers. "The rest we can work out. Ma will come around, I promise."

"I hope so," she replied as she leaned against me.

It wasn't a total wipeout, but I'd take my small victories where I could get them. And "kids" alongside "someday" was a victory I was counting on.

Errands were becoming never-ending. With just a couple months until the wedding and my show on hiatus, Abby elected me to do all of the last-minute running. She was working her ass off so she could take time off in September for the wedding and honeymoon without too much guilt. It wasn't that I minded playing gopher, but it seemed like her list got longer every day. RSVPs came in by the droves and we'd heard back from over half of the people on our invitation list—most of them confirming attendance. Aside from the dress fittings, which thankfully could be passed onto the bridesmaids, everything else was my responsibility. Phillip—The Fabulous—had taken care of most of the details, but since nobody knew our guests like Abby and I did, the seating chart and everything having to do with music fell in our laps. Which meant my lap. Singular. I questioned my sanity incessantly and if I'd had bigger balls, I'd have asked Abby if eloping was an option. I suppose it was my penance for not paying better attention during the earlier stages of planning.

I made a daily run to our post office box to retrieve little ivory RSVP cards by the dozens and I started to wonder just how big that invite list was. I tossed a large stack of mail in the passenger seat and drove home with the hot LA sun beating down through the sun roof. People complained of the heat frequently out here, but after living most of my life on the East Coast, I welcomed it. I had years of snow and slush to make up for.

I pulled in the driveway and drove slowly around to the back of the house. Grabbing the stack of mail and the two bags of groceries from the backseat, I made my way into the house.

Tango met me in a black and white blur, yapping his usual energetic welcome. I gave him a scratch behind the ears, made him shake paws for a treat and opened the sliding door to let him outside. I cranked the stereo and started putting groceries away when I heard banging on the front door. If Tango had burrowed his way underneath the fence again, I was gonna strangle the little mutt. My neighbors' cat was not the least bit amused with Tango's vivacious chases and honestly, I didn't blame him.

I turned down the stereo and headed to the front door, opening it, just in time to see the back of the UPS man retreating down the sidewalk toward his truck. He'd left a giant box in his wake. Jesus, Mary, and Joseph, what the hell did Abby order now?

I picked up the box, expecting it to weigh quite a bit, but I nearly tossed it over my shoulder because of its weightlessness. Looking at the top, I noticed it was addressed to me in familiar handwriting, but the return address was some UPS drop off site in New York. I carried it to the coffee table and grabbed the letter opener off the desk to rip through the tape.

Opening the flaps, I was met with piles and piles of white silk and whatever fabric it is they make ballerina tutus out of. At first glance, it looked like a wedding dress, but Abby's dressmaker was here in California. As I lifted the material out of the box, an ivory card fell to the floor and a small red box became unraveled from the twist of fabric, landing in the bottom of the big box.

As I realized what I was holding, my stomach jumped into my throat.

Carly's dress. *What the fuck*?

I tossed it on the couch and withdrew the red box, knowing without looking that it was the Cartier Asscher diamond I'd bought for her over a decade ago. I fisted the ring, shoved it in my pocket and fell into the chair, speechless. I yanked the ivory card off the floor at my feet and eyed the front. "Carly Cooper" was printed in professional Calligraphic font in the upper left corner of the envelope. My gut churned as I opened it. The "regrets" box was checked with a giant black scrawl and I could only imagine what must've been going through her head when she opened that invitation. I crumpled the RSVP card in my hand and threw it on top of the dress that lie haphazardly across the sofa.

Covering my mouth with my empty hand I just shook my head from side to side in utter confusion. How the hell did Carly get put on the list? I knew I hadn't done it. I cared far too much about her to make her sit through my wedding.

Ma.

I got nauseous at the thought. Surely my mother wouldn't have invited her. I quickly went to the kitchen and grabbed the phone off the counter, dialing Ma and Pop's number by heart. It rang twice before Ma picked it up.

"'ello?"

"Hey Ma," I said. "It's me."

"Joshua? Oh, son, it's so good to hear from you. How are things?" she rattled off her usual greeting.

"Things are fine, Ma." I rattled off mine then realized things were far from fine. "Actually, Ma, things aren't so fine."

"What's the matter?" My mother's immediate response whenever any of us kids admitted to something not being perfectly wonderful in our worlds was panic, and this time was no different. "Are you okay?"

"Yeah, Ma. I'm fine. I just..." I couldn't believe I was about to accuse my mother of such a heinous act, but I had to get to the bottom of this. "Um . . . Ma, when you sent Abby's mom the names and addresses for the wedding, did you . . . um . . . did you include Carly?"

"What?" She sounded shocked. "No! Of course not! Why on earth would you . . . wait . . . what happened?"

I took the ring box out of my pocket and rolled it in my fingers as I told Ma about the delivery.

"Oh sweet Jesus, Joshua."

"Yeaaaah."

"Oh, son," she said, her tone filled with sympathy. "I'm so sorry that happened. But I promise the invitation didn't come from me. I would never do that to our sweet Carly."

"I didn't think so," I replied with heaviness in my voice. "I just had to rule out all options, you know?"

"Well, of course!" she answered. "But, if you didn't invite her, and I didn't invite her, who did?"

"I don't know, Ma." I replied. "Look, I need to go. I need to figure this out. I'll talk to you later."

As I hit the end button on the phone, I looked up and met the eyes of my fiancée. They were wide as she glanced from the couch to the box and then to me. Guilt was written all over her face, and I knew in an instant where Carly's invitation came from.

Quickly, Abby regained her composure and tried feigning innocence. I emphasize "tried".

"What's all that?" she asked, quickly diverting her eyes to the contents of the box.

"You tell me."

"Well, I'm sure I don't know," she said, putting her purse and laptop bag on the sofa table.

"Did you . . ." Blood pumped so hard in my body, I swear I could hear it gush through my veins. "Did you do this?" My voice got a little screechy at the end.

"My God, Josh. Breathe!"

Abby fanned her hands at me, but I was quite done with the bullshit at this point. I took her hands and dragged her to the couch, practically throwing Carly's dress at her. Fabric flapped over her shoulders and part of her face as she caught it.

"DID YOU DO THIS?!" I waved the RSVP card at her furiously. An unfamiliar black rage poured out of me and filled the otherwise silent room. Abby jumped at the volume of my voice, and she began to tear up. I was so angry, I didn't care.

Her eyes fluttered as she struggled to focus.

"ABBY!"

"Yes, Goddamnit!" Her tears spilled over as she threw the dress to the couch and waved her arms angrily. "Carly this and Carly that! Everything since the beginning of our relationship has been about her, and I'm sick of it!"

"What the hell are you talking about?" I snapped. "I haven't brought her up in months!"

"You don't have to," she said. "Your mother does it enough for everybody. All I hear every time I talk to her is how things were 'the last time'. Every damn time, it's 'well, the last time, we invited these people' and 'the last time, they went with a string quartet, not a DJ.' I'm so fucking sick of hearing about 'the last time', Josh! This is *my* time—*our* time. This has nothing to do with Carly, and I wanted to make damn good and sure she knew it."

I stood with one hand on my hip, the other running through my hair, and I was slack-jawed in disbelief. I knew Abby could be catty at times, but this took it to a whole new level. I shook my head, staring into oblivion as I let the depth of Abby's jealousy sink in.

"Well? Aren't you going to say something?" she prodded. "Yell at me some more or tell me what a bitch I am . . . or . . . or . . . something?"

"There's nothing left to say, Abby," I said softly, turning my back on her and shoving my hands in my pockets, feeling the ring box press into my hip like a thorn.

Chapter 9

She didn't say where she was going, but Abby picked up her bags and left the way she came. I heard her tires squeal as her car peeled down the street. At that moment, I didn't even care where she went.

I grabbed a glass, filled it nearly to the brim with scotch and, slamming the door behind me, I went outside to drink and pace as I contemplated what to do. First things first, I had to talk to Carly and make some sort of apology for what had happened. I dialed her number but it went straight to voice mail. I was sure that was on purpose and I didn't blame her. I tried Alejandro next. He answered on the third ring.

"Well hello, asshole!"

I groaned. Of course, he knew.

"I deserved that."

"What the hell were you thinking, man?" Alex's voice had the ability to inflict guilt better than Ma's and that, in itself, was a feat.

"I didn't do it, Alex," I argued. "Abby got all insecure and shit. She invited her. I had no idea she'd even done it until just now."

"Damn, that's cold," he said. "So did Carly call you or what?"

"She didn't tell you?" I was surprised by this. I figured she'd have relayed to Alex the whole dramatic tale. Carly wasn't one to get easily riled, but when she did, shit usually hit the fan, and Alex heard about it within minutes. They'd been that way since high school.

I told him about the delivery then described the fight I'd had with Abby. He let out a low whistle.

"Wow, she must've been pissed," he said. "The dress *and* the ring?"

"Yep."

"What are you gonna do with them?"

"Like I've thought that far ahead, man. I've been too worked up to think about anything yet, but first things, first, I have to deal with this wedding bullshit."

"You're calling it off?"

"Of course! Wouldn't you?"

Alex grumbled under his breath.

"How can I marry someone so insecure and underhanded?"

"Can you really blame her?"

"Who are you, and what have you done with Alejandro?"

"I'm still here," he replied. "I just think you need to look at things from her perspective. I mean, how long has she been living in Carly's shadow?"

"Nice, bro. Now you sound just like her."

"Try and deny it, Josh. Pretend you don't compare everything she is and everything she does to Carly. Shit, man, you probably do it in your sleep! Besides, if you call off another wedding, people are going to start calling you the *Runaway Bride*. And darling, you have way too much body hair to be compared to Julia Roberts."

"You're fucking hysterical, man."

"I say ride it out," he advised. "Abby dealt a low blow, no denying it, but I doubt she wants to call it off. She's just pissed. But, if I'm wrong and she does want to break up then make her do it."

"And let her drag my name through the mud? Hell no!"

"She's gonna swing it however she wants to swing it. Just give things some time to calm down."

Alex had a point. If Abby was so vengeful that she'd send my ex-fiancée an invitation to our wedding then there was no telling what bullshit she'd come up with about me if I called off the wedding. Sadly, there was nothing I could do about it. I could only take Alex's advice and ride it out.

When I hung up with him, I tried Carly's number one more time, but again, it went to voice mail. I threw my phone onto the chair and sat down. I drank in silent contemplation until the stars speckled the sky above me.

Abby and I tiptoed around each other for days, not speaking, not even looking at one another. She'd taken up residence in the guest room at the other end of the upstairs hallway and other than the few times I heard her shower running, it was like I lived alone. We almost had a conversation at dinner one night when I walked into the kitchen and saw her thumbing through an apartment guide, seemingly pricing new housing, but I decided to bite my tongue. Retrieving a cold Corona from the fridge, I returned to my bedroom instead.

Days passed and while neither of us had made a definitive decision regarding the wedding, I think we both knew which direction we were leaning. Unfortunately, Abby didn't have any more balls than I did when it came to actually stepping up to cancel it. We lived in denial, the two of us. It was a sad existence, but I certainly wasn't going to apologize for something that wasn't my fault. Abby stuck to being her normal chin-jerking self whenever she saw me, so I knew she was miles away from an apology. We were at an impasse . . . some sort of fucked-up stalemate.

I refused phone calls from almost everyone, including Phillip, who'd been pressing me constantly about wedding details since Abby had stopped talking to him. Each phone call was more urgent and panicky than the last. My voice mail was full of messages from him, my brother, Abby's mom, and Bobby, who hadn't a clue what was going on except for what Eve told him, which wasn't much. My mother had called once, but thankfully, she knew me well enough to understand my silence and she didn't push for a call-back. I listened to all my messages, but didn't return calls. With the wedding at a standstill, I didn't have a whole lot to say to anyone. Like Alex had suggested, I was leaving that up to Abby.

Rather than fussing over what was supposed to be the happiest time of my life, I submerged myself in music. It had started simply enough weeks before the implosion of my relationship. I'd been trying to write a song to surprise Abby with at our wedding reception. The lyrics had been beautiful and heart-felt, but the accompaniment wasn't coming together like I'd hoped. After the fight, I'd given up and buried the piece under a stack of blank sheet music on the top of the piano. Instead, I wrote sheet after sheet of songs about anger, bitterness, hurt, heartbreak, and betrayal. By the time August rolled around, I had written enough music for a new album, if I'd been so inclined to record them.

I wasn't inclined.

Not in the least.

Okay, maybe a little bit, but only because it took my mind off the wedding bullshit. A few phone calls to my buddies in the music industry could at least get a demo recorded. It couldn't hurt, right? I mean, it wasn't like I had anything else going on. My character on the show had taken a back burner this season, so I wasn't as busy as I'd been earlier this year. I had plenty of time for music if I wanted to do it. I argued with myself quite a bit, but by the end of the first week of August, I convinced myself to make the necessary calls. After that, it was just a waiting game.

Until my world stopped.

The phone woke me up with a jolt. Glancing at the clock as I answered it, my blurry vision made out that it was just after three-thirty. I mumbled a hello, barely recognizing the voice. I heard the words that I'd never wanted to hear, but always knew would come one day.

"Joshua?" Ma's voice sounded from the other end of the line. "Oh, Joshua, he's gone. Your father's gone."

Before the sun began to warm the sky, I booked a private jet and was on my way to Boston. I'd barely had enough forethought to scribble on a Post-It to let Abby know where I'd gone. Even with my scattered thoughts, I made sure to emphasize in my note that I didn't need her there. Given our recent history, I didn't suspect she'd challenge me.

My oldest sister, Maggie met me at the airport, and after a silent, but lengthy embrace we drove to my parents' house in West Roxbury. The rest of my siblings had already converged and were milling around the house along with their spouses and children. Our priest sat talking to my mother as she rocked back and forth in her chair, a dazed stare on her face. As I watched her wrinkled hands stroke the same pattern over and over on her crucifix, I knew she hadn't heard a word Father Brady had said.

"Ma?" I spoke quietly when there was a pause.

"Oh, Joshua!" My mother practically leapt to her feet and into my arms. "My precious boy, what am I going to do?"

"We'll get through it, Ma," I promised. "We'll all get through it together."

The rest of the day was spent arranging my father's funeral. Thankfully, Maggie and my other sisters, Laura and Rebecca, had their wits about them and were able to communicate Ma's hysterical, grief-stricken wishes to the priest and the funeral director. My youngest sister Laura and my brother Matt helped organize the influx of casseroles, cakes, and floral deliveries that had begun to arrive seemingly moments after my father's heart stopped. The house was filled to the rafters with family members and while normally, the crowded rooms would comfort me, I was quickly overwhelmed by it. Everything was all still very surreal to me. Thankfully, I hadn't been assigned any duties yet, except to continue supplying Ma with a fresh handkerchief when the last one became too damp. This was almost all too much to take in, considering what Abby and I had been dealing with back in California just before my mother's phone call. Somehow, though, we got through the first day without any major melt-downs–Ma's not included.

I lay in my old bed that night. The house had dulled to just a low murmur of noise instead of the steady chaos it had been all day. And the gravity of what had happened finally sank in. My chest was heavy with overwhelming grief and deep heartache. Memories of my father flooded my head and I fell asleep wishing for a chance to go back in time.

The following day was spent greeting relatives from every skinny little branch of our giant Irish family tree. It was exhausting to repeat the same conversations over and over again.

"Oh, Josh, we're so sorry..." Yeah? Me, too.

"He was so young..." The man was just a few months away from turning seventy-four. Young? Not so much.

"A heart attack. So sad. So sudden..." Because a long, drawn-out illness would've been so much better?

Of course, I kept my thoughts to myself, but it didn't mean I wanted to. I wanted to scream from the top of the staircase for everyone to go home and pay their respects at the actual funeral on Saturday. I couldn't take two more days of these bullshit condolences that didn't console any of us. It wasn't that we were ungrateful. Obviously, we knew Pop had been loved by many, but didn't people know by now that nothing helped when a family is grieving? Even Ma started getting short with people by noon. She retreated to her bedroom after lunch and left us kids to deal with the aunts, uncles and cousins. I didn't blame her. If anything, I envied her.

Eventually, the crowd thinned out and by the time dinner rolled around, just Matt, Maggie and I were left. Laura and Rebecca had been perfect hostesses and had helped chauffeur family members to their respective hotels nearby. I made a mental note to buy them both a BMW for taking the bullets for the rest of us. Maggie took to writing out a list of names for thank you cards while Matt and I cleaned up the kitchen.

"How you holdin' up, little brother?" he asked me as he handed me a plate to put in the dishwasher.

"Remember that time you got your bike pedal caught in my spokes and we both crashed into the Fitzgeralds' chain link fence? I split my lip and you got that gash across your forehead?"

Matt snorted. "That good, huh?"

"This is worse," I responded dryly.

We were silent a few more minutes, and then Matt asked me the million dollar question.

"So, when is Abby getting in?"

I exhaled sharply and braced myself on the counter. "She isn't."

He stopped and looked at me. I felt his stare practically bore through my skull.

"She isn't coming to Pop's funeral? Is she okay?"

"Yeah."

"Then why isn't she coming?" Christ, this guy and his twenty questions!

"Because I told her not to come!" I yanked the dish towel off my shoulder and chucked it at him, storming into the dining room.

He caught the towel before it hit him in the face and followed me into the other room. I busied myself with picking up dishes and discarded napkins off the table.

"What the hell, Josh? What's going on?" Matt didn't relent. "Why didn't you invite Abby?"

I exhaled sharply, set down the stuff in my hands and braced my hands on the back of a chair. "Because we're calling off the wedding."

"What? Why?"

I hadn't wanted to get into all this, especially now with Pop's funeral just days away, but it didn't seem I had much choice. Damn my brother and his fucking questions. He couldn't just leave well-enough alone.

"Abby sent Carly an invitation to our wedding."

"Whoa . . . wait a minute. What?" Matt's eyes went wide.

I explained briefly about the package from Carly and the confrontation with Abby.

"Oh, man. I'm so sorry," Matt put his arm around my shoulders and squeezed me in a quick hug. "You're seriously calling off the wedding, though?"

"We haven't talked in weeks," I defended. "It's like living in a Chaplin film at my house."

"Want some advice?" Matt asked.

I gave him a flat stare.

"Well, you're getting some anyway," he said. "Look, the wedding is in what, three weeks? Four?"

I nodded.

"If you're going to call it off, you need to do it now. Otherwise, you need to get your ass back to California on Sunday and give it all you've got. Forgive her and move on."

"How the fuck do I forgive her?"

"You just do, man." His voice was matter-of-fact and left little room for argument—not that I really had any to begin with. "Look, bro. You asked her to be your wife—you are committing the rest of your lives together, good, bad and ugly. So? This is ugly. I get it. But she didn't sleep with your best friend. She didn't empty your bank account. She didn't steal your car. There's a lot worse shit she could've done."

I didn't respond. I just let his words tumble around in my head for a minute.

"Just think about it, okay?"

I nodded in reluctant agreement. And for the next three days, to help get my mind off losing Pop, I did as Matt suggested. I knew he was right, in context, at least. But actually forgiving her and making that first step toward amends was a different story. Carly had been an extension of me for so long that Abby's territorial piss had essentially covered my legs, too. If nothing else, Abby should've considered Carly's feelings because *I* considered Carly's feelings. That part was hard to get past.

Chapter 10

On Saturday, before the funeral, I paced back and forth in the vestibule of the church. I was no closer to being able to let go of my father than I was to letting go of my anger toward Abby. Mourners and curious church goers shuffled in, giving me silent nods as they passed. I nodded back occasionally but acknowledged no one out loud.

Ma and my sisters had set up camp in one of the holding rooms until the service. By now, my mother had had her fill of well-meaning relatives, especially after Pop's wake the night before. At this point, she just wanted to bury my father and retreat to a quiet place again. Matt, God bless the poor bastard, had taken it upon himself to stand with Father Brady at the doors, offering handshakes and accepting words of condolence from those who entered the sanctuary. It was more than I could take, hence my retreat to the far end of the vestibule.

I could've used Alejandro's sarcasm right about then, but some work thing had kept him from coming. Instead, he sent an obscenely enormous flower arrangement and a fifteen-year-old bottle of Glenfiddich to try and make up for his absence. Turning my back to the door, I stole a nip from my father's flask, which I'd confiscated the day before from his liquor cabinet. Alex's scotch couldn't get me through the day, but it was better than nothing. I spun the cap back on and slipped it back into the breast pocket of my jacket. I shook my arms and hands out, inhaled a couple of quick deep breaths, and turned around.

My eyes met hers and my heart dropped into my stomach.

Shit.

Carly stood about twenty feet away looking like a runway model. She wore a sleek black dress that hugged her curves perfectly but not intentionally. The only hint of color was a light blue headband holding back her mane of curls. Carly never did understand the effect she had on others. All the time she thought she was dressing conservatively, she was turning heads left and right. Even today, her black stockings and high heels were more than I could take. How the hell could she awaken the beast today of all days?

She gave a small nod my way. As I took the first step toward her, a man stepped up beside her and put his hand on the lower part of her back while he whispered something in her ear. She turned toward him and gave him a smile I recognized. I'd been given that smile more times than I could count. They were a couple. No doubt about it.

And just like that butterflies in my stomach that fluttered at the sight of her turned to a swarm of bees stinging me from the inside out. I gulped hard, clenched my fists a couple times, and somehow drummed up the courage to greet her. Each step felt like I was walking on hot coals.

"Carly," I mumbled. "It's . . . it's good to see you." I managed to kiss her cheek without throwing her over my shoulder in some caveman gesture of assholery. "You look good."

"Thanks. So do you." Her nervousness showed, but ever the lady, she made introductions. "Josh, this is Trey Foster."

The man extended his hand with a smile. "Josh, I've heard a lot about you. It's a pleasure to meet you; I'm sorry it's under these circumstances." He was a tall, dark-skinned man with a smile that outshined mine tenfold. His black suit was tailored perfectly, and his gray dress shirt crisp with starch. I pretended not to notice his powder blue tie that matched Carly's headband as I shook his hand politely. I wanted to deck him, but I knew that it wasn't the time or place. I did, however, let my stare bore through his until he looked away uncomfortably.

You could cut the awkwardness with a knife; I prayed for a freak lightning storm to strike the church and relieve us all from the discomfort.

"Carly? Darling, is that you?" My mother's voice echoed through the vestibule and I said a silent prayer of thanks. Ma wasn't a lightning storm, but she'd do. She rushed over to Carly and enveloped her in a hug. After introductions, she also embraced Trey like she'd known him for years. Abby, she practically excommunicated from the Holy Church of McCarthy, but this guy she welcomed with open arms? *Traitor.*

I excused myself, feigning a quick need to talk to the priest. Ma nodded, slipped Carly's hand in the crook of her arm, and showed the two of them to their seats inside the sanctuary. I watched them, dumbfounded, as Ma led them to their pew and stood talking to them for longer than what I felt was necessary.

I took a couple of deep breaths and scrubbed my hand over my face before joining Matt and Father Brady. I was on autopilot for the next few minutes while greeting latecomers before Father Brady left to herd the acolytes to prepare for the ceremony.

"So," Matt said, "She showed up."

"Yep."

"That's a little weird."

"Yep."

"You okay?"

"Yep."

"Want me to distract her while you stab the dude?"

"Ha!" I snorted. "Yeah, that'd be great. Thanks, man."

He patted my shoulder and gave me an encouraging squeeze.

"C'mon, baby brother. It's not going to get any easier."

He was right. It didn't get any easier.

Ma had come to me earlier in the week to ask if I would sing at the service. I'd fought her hard, but she knew I could never tell her no. After Father Brady delivered the liturgy, I squeezed Ma's hand and walked to the pulpit. I'd performed thousands of times in my life, but never for something like this. Never to honor someone I loved.

I cleared my throat, took a glance at my father's casket, and closed my eyes, letting the first words of the song flow out of me.

"And now, the end is here..." I began in a shaky voice.

Sinatra probably wasn't the Vatican's first choice for funeral songs, but I'd say my Hail Mary's later. My voice steadied with each measure and, unaccompanied, echoed through the church with resounding impact. As the song went on, I let the tears fall, letting out the grief I'd been holding in all week. By the end of the song, the lapels of my suit jacket were damp, and I knew there wasn't a dry eye in the house.

Without a word, I stepped from the altar, leaned down and kissed my father's coffin, before walking slowly back to my seat next to my mother.

I don't remember much else about the service or the interment afterward. I went through the motions: hugging, praying, accepting condolences.

By the time the last prayer was said, I was ready to go.

Unfortunately, there was one last thing I had to do, which I'd forgotten about until she walked up to me as I was helping Ma back to the car.

"Josh, I'm sorry about your dad," Carly said, clutching a handkerchief with tear stains on her cheeks. "He was a good man and I loved him very much." She paused, as if not sure what else to say. She followed the pause with a hug and I had to force myself not to hang onto her.

"Thank you, Carly," I replied, praying silently that she'd let go first. I knew I couldn't.

"We better be going, Babygirl," Trey urged, touching her elbow causing her to pull away from me.

Babygirl? Where did he get off? She was my *Beautiful*, not his *Babygirl*. Schmuck in his matchy-matchy tie. I wasn't sure if the sneer I made was just in my head or not.

"Of course," she nodded.

"I'm very sorry about your father, Josh," Trey said.

"Thanks," I replied blankly.

"If you need anything, please don't hesitate." Carly offered, as everyone had offered a thousand times over that day.

And, just like I did to everyone else that day, I simply pursed my lips and nodded in gratitude.

By the time I turned my light off that night, a ball of stone had formed in my gut. The same rock I'd felt a thousand times over whenever I thought about Carly over the last year. I was so sick of hurting whenever she came to mind. I just wanted to move on, and after today, I thought I'd had just enough to do that very thing.

After a mechanical delay and a four-hour unscheduled layover in Chicago, I finally made it to Los Angeles after eleven on Sunday night. I grabbed my carry-on and trudged my way down the tiled hallways to the baggage claim for my suitcase. I was physically and emotionally exhausted, and despite the sun having set hours ago, I kept my sunglasses on to cover the dark circles and bags under my eyes. Obviously, I wasn't paying attention to anyone around me. Instead, I scrolled through text messages as I waited for the belt to fire to life.

"Need a ride, mister?" a voice brought me out of my zone. I glanced up and there stood Abby. She was absent of make-up, her hair windblown and half-hanging in her face. She wore a ratty t-shirt, jean shorts and some threadbare sandals. And in this raw, natural state, she was the most beautiful sight I'd ever seen.

"How did you..."

"I called your mom's house and talked to Matt. He told me when your flight was," she explained. "I've been here since six waiting for you."

I stood slack-jawed for a moment then dropped my bag and pulled her into my arms.

"Josh, I'm sorry," she blurted out as she hugged me tightly. "I'm sorry for everything. For the invitation, for the jealousy, for not coming to Boston . . . for all of it. I'm so, so sorry. Please forgive me."

"Forget it," I dismissed her, kissing her lips, cheek and side of her head repeatedly. I was so weary from hanging onto the past—hanging onto Carly, specifically. It was time to move forward and this was the only way I could do it. "None of it matters now, Abby. You're here and that's what counts."

I pulled back long enough to smooth her hair back from her face, and look at her to make sure she was real before kissing her again. I'd never felt so relieved in my life. It was then that I knew I would marry her. Damn the invitation, damn the dress, damn the ring. Damn it all to hell. I loved this woman, and that's all there was to it.

Epilogue

"Good morning, Mrs. McCarthy," I whispered to my sleeping bride who lay haphazardly next to me in the king-sized bed overlooking the Arabian Sea. Our little Maldivian bunker stood on several wooden stilts just a few feet over the salt water beneath us. It lapped at the pillars rhythmically all night, setting a most pleasant pattern for REM when our insatiable bodies finally gave up feasting on each other.

"Mmmm," she purred. "Good morning, Mr. McCarthy." She stretched her long legs and slithered one between mine as she turned toward me. Her long hair still held its curl from the day before and the scent of gardenias from her bouquet still clung to her skin.

"How'd you sleep, angel?" I peppered her face with kisses.

"You mean after you molested me every legal way imaginable?" She giggled.

"And probably a few illegal ones," I added, as I leaned down and circled my lips around her nipple, giving it a firm suck. She squealed and laughed again.

"I love you, Josh."

"I love you, too."

And I sincerely did. Abby was the polar opposite of Carly in every way and she was good for me. Even Ma said as much at the wedding. She said Abby was exactly what I needed right now, and she was right.

The wedding had been beautiful and went off without a hitch. Insanely expensive, mind you, but perfect in every way. As planned, her parents refused to let us pay for any of it. I didn't feel right about that part, but the Levys insisted. And once I saw the open bar bill after my Irish Catholic relatives raided it, I didn't envy my father-in-law for having to write that check.

Pop was obviously missed, but he was there in spirit. Ma was her typical emotional self, especially without having my father there to help talk her off the ledge. But my brother and Alejandro snuck Kahlua in her coffee all night and by the time we cut the cake, she was three sheets to the wind and didn't care about anything except dancing.

Abby's family was a bit more conservative in that respect, but they, too, had a good time. My mother-in-law made a lasting impression when the back of her dress got caught in her panty hose in the bathroom: she gave my uncle's table a view of her liposuctioned ass when she came out, but she laughed it off with Abby's assistance in making light of it.

Abby gave me a kiss, bringing me back to the present before crawling out of bed and heading toward the bathroom. My eyes followed her. She was the most beautiful woman I'd ever known and at that moment, I felt like the luckiest man alive to be married to her.

Acknowledgements

Let me just start off by saying that my beta readers are the best! You ladies got a very raw product—typos, misspellings, and all—and helped me sculpt it into a cohesive story that made sense. Thank you, Ann Marie, Peggy, Wendy, Yoly and Laura.

To the numerous bloggers who have featured my work—how wonderful are you?! I love that you love my characters as much as I do. On behalf of myself and other authors, I thank you for all the time and energy you spend supporting us. You are priceless!

Jacquelyn Ayres, you're my angel. Besides being a remarkable editor for Josh's story, you've kept me upright and breathing these last few months. When I was ready to throw in the towel, you reminded me I wasn't alone in this. Thank you for our countless conversations, your vast knowledge of *The Chicago Manual of Style*, and for drinking the wine I can't have. I am so lucky to have you as a friend!

I'm sending a cape and an invisible plane to my friend, Cynthia Hill. Not only do you work a full-time job, take care of your family, and manage your *own* writing career, you didn't hesitate to jump in when you saw me flailing in the deep end. Thank you so much for all your help with this project.

DeLaine Roberts, my darling, I literally could not have done this without you. You jumped into this thing at the last minute without hesitation and delivered a flawless product. You're a formatting genius, and I am so grateful to be working with you!

They say you shouldn't judge a book by its cover, but I beg you—judge, away! If my book is half as good as its cover, then it's one hell of a story. Kim Crecelius, you came through for me again. The cover is gorgeous! I love it, and I love you. I thank you so much for sticking with me, juggling your schedule, and dealing with my impatience. I am eternally indebted to you.

I've always dreamed about getting an autograph from boy bander. Instead, a boy bander ended up with mine. How does that even happen?! When Jeff Timmons asked me for a copy of *Distance and Time*, I thought he was joking. After all, we razz each other a lot. He *wasn't* kidding, and somehow, my sweet, little romance novel ended up in his hands—I'm still trying to figure it out. Jeff, I hope my stories have done justice to the life that you and other artists lead. You have my everlasting admiration for going out and doing the things I can only write about.

Next, I applaud *you*, my fans, friends, and family. Whether you saw this book in its early stages, read an advanced copy—still riddled with errors—or just finished the epilogue a couple minutes ago, *you* are the reason I write. Without you, these stories would still be tucked away in my head. Not only have you breathed life into my characters, you've rooted for them . . . and for me. From buying my book (sometimes, multiple copies!) to pimping me out to your hairdressers, I couldn't ask for a greater support system. You are the cornerstone of my success.

Lastly, but certainly not least, I thank Wendy and Claire at *Bare Naked Words* for taking me on and helping lead the way through the promotion and touring phase of this series. You two have been relentlessly diligent. Thank you for believing in my work and pushing it so hard on my behalf. I don't know where I'd be without you!

More From The Author

About the Author

Mel Henry has been an avid reader since stealing her first *Harlequin* from her mom's nightstand in second grade. Because some words were too big for her seven-year-old vocabulary, she took to writing her own stories (much to the relief of her teacher) and has been doing so ever since.

After having held various jobs in her life that brought her no satisfaction and only a piddly income, she decided to publish her first book. She figured being a starving artist instead of just starving sounded much more interesting. Being able to do it in her pajamas and without make-up are just perks to the job.

Living in Iowa with her husband and two teenaged daughters, Mel's an avid cook (sometimes by choice), seasoned traveler (always by choice), and a hardcore warrior against chronic Lyme disease (definitely not by choice). She loves live theater, thunderstorms, and good tea. She loathes conspiracy theories, egotistical people, and sushi.

Better in Time is Mel's second novel. She is currently collaborating with three other authors on a project, and has the foundation in place for her next series. In the meantime, you can find her current works or stalk her at:

www.amazon.com

www.barnesandnoble.com

www.kobo.com
www.itunes.com
www.twitter.com/mel_henry
www.mellysramblings.blogspot.com
www.facebook.com/melhenryauthor
mel.henry@ymail.com

An excerpt from

All This Time

Time After Time series, volume 3

the sequel novel to *Distance and Time*

~unedited~

Prologue

April 1994

Diary entry

My life is a mess. Everything I thought I knew is wrong, and I don't know where to begin rebuilding. As much as I'd like to blame the South Station phenomenon for the chaos, I know it has nothing to do with that. The fans are nuts—don't get me wrong, but they aren't the downfall of my relationship with Josh. I could even blame that blonde bitch Jenna if I wanted to, but I can't. If Josh tells me there's nothing going on, then I believe him. After all, I've been behind the scenes and I see how things can be twisted by the media. Pure and simple, we are at different places in our lives. While I sit here in my dorm at NYU, he's on a tour bus somewhere in Australia. Or is it Asia? Hell, I don't even know. I don't know why I thought it could work, anyway. I was fooling myself.

I just reread the last letter Josh sent me over and over again, looking for obvious clues I missed the first sixty times I read it. Just like the last time, I didn't find any. The letter is full of "miss you's" and "I can't wait 'til we're together again's" and he signed it, "Love, Josh." He talked about the tough tour schedule and he mentioned looking for new management, but where "we" are concerned, everything looks fine.

My relationship with Josh McCarthy was something that pretty much fell into my lap. I was on a college visit at Northwestern and ran into Josh and his bandmate, Marc Reyes at a club when I was with some friends. He invited me to a baseball game the next afternoon, and things bloomed from there. We spent the last year loving each other from a distance and up close.

My best friend Alejandro was one of the few people who supported our union. Alex Cruz was a big fan of South Station Boyz, too and loved that one of us was dating a member of the group. In fact, when Josh wanted to surprise me at Prom, he and Alex worked together to make it happen.

From that point on, they were best buds. Together, we were like the Three Musketeers.

South Station Boyz had a loyal following, affectionately known in the media as "Trainwreckz." They were many of them who lived up to that moniker. Even at my own school, I was taunted by girls claiming that Josh was their boyfriend and that I better step off if I knew what was good for me. For obvious reasons, I went out of my way to lie low where my adoration for Josh and the band was concerned. He reminded me more than once that we knew the truth, and that is what mattered.

Josh told me later that he noticed me the minute I walked in the club that night— that his eyes gravitated toward me. He had watched me for a while before he decided he had to meet me, claiming that my smile intrigued him. The whole night was a blur, but I will always remember what it felt like to be in his arms on that dance floor.

I've forgotten the first song we danced to, but I remember him holding me close to him. Not so close that he couldn't make me melt with those baby blues of his, though. Josh was all smiles. Eyes and smiles. And a smooth tenor voice that sang along with every word of the songs we danced to. It was a triple threat of sexy if there ever was one. He complimented my outfit—a carefully constructed ensemble my friends had put together before we left my hotel that night. He commented on my hair, twisting a stray brunette curl around his finger at random. He nearly purred in my ear when he mentioned how good my perfume smelled. We danced to that song and every other song after that until his bandmate Marc literally came and pulled him away.

We agreed to meet up the next day and from there, I was hooked. I had my doubts, of course. My self-esteem had taken quite a beating over the years at the hands of my step-dad, and my confidence frequently waivered, because of it. I wondered what Josh saw in me and, while I didn't often vocalize my fears, I questioned his decision to be with me. As time went on, I learned to trust him, and I began believing the compliments he gave me. He was good for my spirit, and our relationship was all I'd ever dreamed it could be.

But something changed.

We don't talk on the phone anymore. He hasn't mentioned coming to see me when tour is done next month or talked about me visiting him. He hasn't brought up spending any time together this summer. In fact, he hasn't mentioned anything about us in a long time. I feel like a war bride. I keep waiting for someone to show up with a telegram to tell me our relationship has been killed in action. To quote that John Cusack movie we watched one time, "I gave her my heart and she gave me a pen." I'd given Josh my heart (among other body parts), and in return I got to say I dated a member of South Station Boyz. Yeah, that was a fair trade. I grunted in disgust at myself and the situation. Looking down at my diary, I continued writing.

The thing is, even for as crappy as I feel, I can't help thinking that I lived a dream thousands of girls would die for. I don't hate him. Hell, I'm not even angry at him. I miss him, don't get me wrong. And my heart aches like it's never ached before, but I can't help feeling like this isn't the end. Am I just being naïve? I guess time will tell.

Until then, I have to put my energy into school.

20339780R00086

Made in the USA
San Bernardino, CA
07 April 2015